Edge
of
Ready

L.B. Tillit

SADDLEBACK
EDUCATIONAL PUBLISHING

GRAVEL ROAD

Edge of Ready
Unchained
2 Days

SADDLEBACK
EDUCATIONAL PUBLISHING
www.sdlback.com

ISBN-13: 978-1-61651-778-6
ISBN-10: 1-61651-778-6
eBook: 978-1-61247-381-9

Printed in Guangzhou, China
1111/CA21101774

16 15 14 13 12   1 2 3 4 5

Sometimes we find ourselves on a gravel road, not sure of how we got there or where the road leads. Sharp stones pellet the unprotected. And the everyday wear and tear sears more deeply. Saddleback's series, Gravel Road, highlights the talents of our urban street lit authors.

ACKNOWLEDGMENTS

I would like to thank Aaron Thompson, Steve Woodson, Mack McKeller, and Rhoda Ricciardi for sharing their knowledge concerning criminal justice. Thanks to my children, Sarah, Amy, and Maya, my husband, Tore, my parents, Keith and Jonlyn, and my sister Kym for their support in writing this first book. Additional thanks to Anne Wanicka, my mentor and friend.

My greatest gratitude goes to my students whose true stories remain more unbelievable than fiction. They are my heroes.

CHAPTER 1

Dani

I should have never been born. That's what my daddy said before he shut the door. I never saw him again.

True, I was only three, but I can still see his long black hair fall into his face. He pushed it back with one hand as he opened the door with the other. He spit words out in Spanish. I don't know what he said, but Mom cried and yelled, "You better not come back." So he didn't.

Mom took me in her arms. Her skin looked black against my chubby brown legs. She said we could do this, just the two of us. I believed her.

We moved a week later. Mom said we didn't need three bedrooms. She said smaller was better. I believed her.

By the time I was seventeen I knew she had lied. We moved because she didn't want Daddy to find us. She also needed a cheap place.

But I didn't care. West Street was my home and I was just happy to have my own room while Mom shared her room with Benny. Benny is my baby brother. When I was sixteen Mom thought she had a thing going with her white boss at Ted's Rest Hotel across town. It was going to move us out of here. The minute he found out Benny was on the way it was over. Mom cried for weeks. She cried, "We're stuck!"

I just held her and said, "Mom, why do you want to get out?" When she didn't speak I said, "You always said this was better than where we were before."

"You're right, Dani." She took my hand and wiped her tears. "It is better. I just want more for you, baby."

"More?" I looked at my mom. Her dark skin was smooth and beautiful. She didn't have a muffin top like I did. I kept waiting for my baby fat to go away. I was in for a long wait. I would never look like Mom. I could see why men liked her. Why they wanted her. But for the first time I saw some gray beginning to color her hair.

"You got to finish school!" Mom looked at me as I rolled my eyes. She always went back to the school thing. "Dani Garcia, don't you roll your eyes at me!" She pointed her finger in my face. "You want to be stupid and let others decide for you?"

"No, Mom," I said, just like always. She looked at me and smiled.

"Whatever happens, school comes first!" Mom said it like she meant it. I believed her.

Then along came Benny. His blue eyes shocked both of us. So I called him my white brother. I guess he's not much whiter than me since my dad was Hispanic.

I hated it when people tried to talk Spanish with me since I didn't know any. Just because I looked like a Garcia didn't mean I could *say* anything. Kids teased me when I was younger, calling me stupid. They backed off when I learned to cuss them out in Spanish. They didn't ask me to speak Spanish again.

At seventeen I was facing my last year of school. I was facing graduation. Easy, right? Wrong!

CHAPTER 2

Ruth

Ruth was my best friend. She had been since we moved to West Street. It was easy to be her friend. She lived in the same building, and we went to school together. She never teased me about my dad being Hispanic. Maybe that's why I liked her.

As we grew together, we stayed friends. But when we were twelve I could tell she was more into boys than I was. She would say, "Come on, Dani! Chris likes you. Come on, kiss him! It feels real good." I hated Chris, a neighbor who was twice as fat as me. I guess Ruth thought we made a pair. She thought wrong. I could see him staring at me, and I would just want to puke.

"I want to kiss someone I love!" I would say to Ruth. She would look at me and laugh.

"You stupid! Boys don't love you. They just want you!" She'd punch me and I'd tell her to shut up.

Still we were friends. She never teased me about finishing school. I think she told people she stayed in school to watch my back. But really she stayed because she liked boys. She liked boys wanting her. She didn't mind letting them have her.

Still, we were friends.

CHAPTER 3

Evron and Keon

Most of my world seemed to have a phone, so I asked Mom if I could have one too. Since Benny was born Mom did want to reach me when she needed to. So she bought me a cell phone with prepaid minutes. Mom chewed me out because I used up my whole $20 card in one day talking to Ruth. Mom told me we didn't have money to burn and she asked why I was talking to Ruth on the phone when I could just go over to her house. So that's what I did.

Ruth had two brothers. At eighteen Evron was beautiful, if you can call a boy beautiful. His skinny teen years were over. I liked it when he showed off his six pack. His black skin was so smooth that I longed to reach out and see if his beauty would rub off on me. But he never looked at me. When I was with Ruth he'd come and go without saying a word.

But Keon, who was two years older, always talked to me. He was tall and not bad to look at either. His hair was so short he looked like he was in the army. He said he packed meat at the Market Place and had to keep a clean cut. I think he made it up, but it made him feel big.

Keon was the only one in the family that had graduated. He made sure everyone knew it, and he always told Ruth she better not drop out. Not like Evron. Ruth said they'd never make it without Keon's paycheck since their father left.

Their mother and Keon worked all the time while Evron just liked to hang out all day. He spent a lot of time on his phone. He liked to show off how fast he could text. I wanted to believe he was just hanging out and texting with friends, but deep down I knew better. There was no way he could look so hot in his clothes. There was no way he could pay for his phone without some extra money coming in. I just pushed the thought away.

It was Saturday. We had just finished our first week back at school. I was hanging out at Ruth's. Like always, Saturday was spent on her couch watching TV. When the boys were younger they'd watch TV too. But mostly they were gone. That morning was different. That morning the boys were home.

"So it's your senior year?" Keon asked me as he took a sip of Pepsi.

I sat down on the couch with him and smiled, "Yeah. I can't believe it." I turned to see if Evron had already left.

When I looked back, I saw Keon frown. He pushed the look away and took another sip. "So you gonna make it?"

I stopped smiling. "What's that mean?"

Just then Evron walked through the bedroom door. He stopped before he got to the front door and looked at me. *He* looked at *me*. He looked at me. My heart stopped. He winked and then left. I looked at the closed door and smiled.

"That's what I mean!" Keon jumped up and walked into the bedroom. He slammed the door. I sat there dazed. What had just happened?

"Don't worry about Keon!" Ruth said as she plopped down next to me. "He's like the dad around here." She smiled and said, "I think Evron is checkin' you out." She tried to reach to pinch my cheek, but I slapped her hand.

Soon we both started to giggle like little girls. I couldn't help but whisper into Ruth's ear. "Your brother's so fine!" She knew which one I was talking about.

CHAPTER 4

September

The first month of school was okay. My English class was hard, but I knew I was almost done with school. I could push through any hard classes. Mrs. Grady pulled me aside after class one day. Her little white self got up really close. I could smell the smoke on her. The wrinkles just spread wide into a smile. "Now Dani, hon, you're doing really well."

"Thanks, Mrs. Grady," I smiled and stepped back. Her breath just about knocked me out.

The old lady stepped in again. "Tell me, dear. How is your mother?"

I stepped away again. I could tell she dyed her hair red, really red. "Fine." I was short and sweet. Why did she want to know anyway?

The smile faded for a moment. It was like she was thinking. She was trying to come up with something else to say. I finally started to turn and go. I felt her hand on my arm, "Dani?" She was smiling again, but it was not the same. "I heard she had a baby."

I looked at her funny. "So?" I didn't mean to be rude, but there it was.

"Oh, dear," Mrs. Grady shook her head. "I didn't mean to upset you. I just want you to keep doing your best."

Something hurt deep down. Wasn't I always doing my best? Why did people keep making me feel like I might not make it? I looked at her and tried to be nice, but my edge was still there. "Ma'am, I think I have shown I can do it. Thank you, but it really is none of your concern." As I turned to leave I saw Mrs. Grady look at me. I couldn't help feeling that she knew something I didn't know.

CHAPTER 5

October

Benny was five months old when he started to crawl. Well, sort of. He would pull up on his elbows and scoot. He looked funny. Butt up and then elbows, scoot, then butt down. Looked like a baby version of the worm. I was laughing and smiling, which just made Benny look at me. His blue eyes would twinkle. He was so proud. "Mom, you've got to see this!" I yelled to mom who was putting frozen pizza in the microwave.

She turned around and smiled at Benny's crawl, but then she stopped. "Oh, no! Not yet!" She looked at me, almost dropping the pizza. Of course I looked at her like she must be crazy. Who ever heard of a mother not happy to see her baby crawl? "Dani, it's—you didn't crawl until ten months!"

"So? This is great news then. Benny is really doing great." I grabbed Benny and held him. He started patting my face and sticking his hand in my mouth.

Mom finally got the pizza in the microwave and turned it on. She crossed to the couch and sat down. "I know. I am happy. But Mrs. Carson likes babies that don't move much."

"What?" I didn't get it. Mrs. Carson was our neighbor who was watching Benny while Mom was at work and I was at school. She seemed nice enough.

Mom just shook her head. "Yeah, soon she'll start finding reasons why she can't watch Benny. She just doesn't want kids messing with her stuff."

"Why did you put Benny with her in the first place?" I put Benny back down on the floor.

Mom moved in closer to her boy. "Because it was easy. She's right next door. Now I've got to start looking for a permanent baby-sitter."

My stomach hurt. I asked Mom a question I already knew the answer to, "So, you have someone in mind. Right?" She didn't look at me. She waited. Then she slowly shook her head.

"Mom!" I yelled. "Why not?"

"Dani!" She raised her voice. "Don't you yell at me. How could I know he would crawl so soon?"

I stood up and started walking around the small room. "So what do we do?"

"Well, Mrs. Carson hasn't said anything yet. So we don't need to worry. I'll start looking tomorrow." Mom finally looked at me. "Okay, Dani?" She got back up and headed to the kitchen. The pizza wasn't done yet, but it didn't matter.

I just shook my head. I knew it would be up to me. I knew if Mom couldn't find someone it would be me. I knew Mom's promise of school coming first was a lie. I stomped to my room and yelled, "Whatever!"

CHAPTER 6
Sweet Candy

Halloween was always the best time of year. It didn't matter how old we were; we always wore fangs or a cape or fake blood. And then there was candy. Sweet candy.

When I was little, Mom said she had to go through the candy bag first before I could. She had to make sure the candy was safe. I would just say, "Sure, Mom." And then I'd stand there and watch her pick out the candy she wanted. She'd smile with chocolate between her teeth when she handed the bag back to me. I would always say, "Dress up yourself next time!" Then I would find a place to sit and finally enjoy what was left.

For Halloween I dressed Benny up as a bunny. Cute! I spent Halloween afternoon on the bus getting to the mall and back with Benny all dressed up. It went as planned. My bag, I mean Benny's bag, was full of candy that the stores gave out. They would put candy in the bag with one hand as they pinched Benny's cheek with the other hand.

Before I went to our apartment I knew I could hit up the old ladies in our building, and they would just spill out the candy. But I was wrong. It looked like less people answered their doors this year. I decided to stop by Ruth's place to show her Benny before I headed home.

Evron answered the door. "Hello there." His eyes were sleepy.

"Did I wake you?" I said, turning to go.

"Nah, just watchin' TV." He touched my arm and pulled me into the stuffy room. The TV was loud. "Cute Bunny." Evron pulled Benny's bunny ear. Benny giggled.

"Yeah. It's his first Halloween and all," I smiled.

Evron looked at me. "Does he eat candy already?"

I turned red. I suddenly felt fat and childish. I just shook my head, no.

Big white teeth smiled at me. He grabbed the candy bag and jumped on the couch. "Let's see what you got."

I started to go for the bag, but I felt stupid. "Is Ruth here?" I finally asked. "I wanted her to see Benny."

"Ruth!" Evron yelled over the TV. "Dani's here!"

As I waited for Ruth, I realized that that was the first time I ever heard Evron say my name. I smiled, just a little. He looked at me smile and smiled back. Suddenly I was red again.

"Aw! He's so cute!" Ruth ran up to me and grabbed Benny. I couldn't help notice Evron was still looking at me.

We hung out just a little while before I decided I better head home. As I reached the door I heard Evron get up from the couch. "Wait. You forgot this." He walked right up to me with the very full bag. He handed it to me. He held on to it for just a little longer as he said, "I like your candy." I could feel my body heat rise.

CHAPTER 7

November

Mrs. Grady was nicer than ever. She seemed more into my grades than ever. She asked about my family more than ever. Strange. But it made English class a little better. She seemed to think what I said mattered. So I really tried. I was making an A.

But then Benny really started crawling. And Mrs. Carson called. She couldn't watch Benny anymore.

I remember the first day I missed class. It wasn't great at all. I think that was what everyone thought. "I bet Dani's glad. She's got a reason to skip." But it felt like a deep pit in my stomach. It was like a hole I was afraid I wasn't going to be able to climb out of.

"It's just today," Mom said as she saw the look of fear on my face. She looked at me really hard. "I need you to not make a bigger deal about this than it is." I just stared. "What?" She raised her voice. "Do you think I should stay here instead?"

I looked down and the words came out before I could stop them. "Well, he is *your* baby."

Mom came right up on me. Her finger was in my face. Her voice was hard and cold. "Dani Tiana Garcia who do you think you are? This is my home, my food, and my clothes. I pay for every last bit of it. It's time you do your part."

Our eyes locked as I dared to ask, "But Mom, what about school? You said …"

"I know what I said!" Mom shook her head and looked at me with sad eyes. She knew I was right, but she had no choice. I had no choice. "We'll talk about this later! I've got to get to work. Sheets don't wash themselves." She stopped and looked at me again. She didn't yell anymore. "It's just today. I'll see if Mrs. Parks can help out." I nodded and let her go.

All day I tried to think it would just be one day. But I knew better. I would look at Benny and yell, "I hate you!"

But he would crawl over to me and look at me with his big blue eyes and say, "Ni, Ni" with his arms held up until I held him and kissed him.

To my shock, Mom did get Mrs. Parks to watch Benny the next day. I guessed Mom remembered her promise.

CHAPTER 8

Too Fast

It happened so fast. It had only been two weeks since Halloween. Ruth and I were on our way home from school. I held open the door to our apartment building. As Ruth stepped in front of me to go inside, she turned to look at me. I didn't think anything of it. She was always stopping before I could completely get through the door. She would cause it to slam into my back. She would laugh as I chased her up the stairs. But not that day. Ruth asked me to come by her place. "It will only take a minute." She smiled really big. "I have a surprise for you."

"Ruth, you know I got to get Benny," I said, not thinking much about it. I headed for the first step.

But Ruth didn't take no for an answer. She quickly came up behind me. "Come on!" She pulled my arm. "Don't you want to see your surprise?"

"Yeah, sure! But I have to get Benny first and then I'll come." I really didn't think that would be a problem. But she suddenly looked really strange. So I asked, "What's wrong?"

Ruth didn't say anything, like she was thinking. Then she whispered, "I guess I can watch Benny."

"What?" I was so confused. "I always bring Benny. What do you mean you'll watch him?"

That's when Ruth had that smile again. "You'll see." That time my stomach felt weird. I shook off the feeling and ran up the steps to my apartment. I knew if I ran up the stairs enough times I would burn some of my fat. Ruth never wanted to and thought it was stupid. She yelled after me, "Don't get too sweaty." Since when did that matter? It only took a few minutes to put down my books and grab Benny. We headed to Ruth's apartment.

I should have not gone. But I did. I should have not gone in the back bedroom with Evron. But I did. It should have made me feel beautiful. But it didn't.

Something changed in me that day. Some people might say, "Oh, you became a woman." But that wasn't it. I didn't feel like a woman. A woman is strong. A woman knows what she wants and how to make it happen. A woman is beautiful. I didn't feel like a woman.

CHAPTER 9
Caught

I was stupid to think one time was it. Evron or Ruth would text me each day. Ruth seemed to think it was all a game. She would always "surprise" me with Evron whenever we went to her house. I would say I didn't want to go, but that just made Ruth mad. "What? You don't want to be friends?" She looked at me all sad. We climbed the stairs together. I didn't feel like running up them anymore.

"No, it's just Evron always wants me to take off with him," I said as I pushed open the door to our apartment. "I think I'll just stay home with Benny today."

"Whatever!" Ruth just turned and started up the stairs. Then she looked at me again. "I thought you wanted a boyfriend."

I shook my head. I didn't know if I should tell her or not, but she was my friend. My best friend. Whatever that meant. I looked at her hoping she would see my pain. "Yeah, but he just sweet talks me for five minutes and then he doesn't talk to me when it's over." I felt stupid trying to explain something I really didn't understand. I didn't know how it was supposed to be. I just knew it wasn't supposed to be like this.

Ruth smiled and came back to me. "Aw, Dani! You just need to give him time. I'll talk to him for you." She turned to go before I could stop her. I didn't want her to talk to Evron. I didn't want Evron to want me. I laughed just a little. Who knew I would ever think that? He was beautiful, but he sure wasn't good at giving me what I needed. I wasn't sure what I needed. I knew it wasn't Evron.

I closed the door and started playing with Benny. I didn't pick up my phone when I heard a text come in. I knew who it was. I started to wish I didn't have a phone.

I had the TV going when I heard the doorbell ring. It was loud and long. I ran to the door, thinking it was Mom coming home early with groceries in her hands. But it wasn't.

It was Evron. His shirt was off and he was only wearing sweats. They were almost falling off of him. His feet were bare. He leaned into me, "Hey, baby. I missed you. You lose your phone? Why you not talking to me?" Evron pulled me close. I didn't like him calling me baby. Only Mom called me baby.

"Hey, Benny is here." I tried to push him back into the hall. But that didn't work.

"It don't matter, baby." Evron shoved the door closed with his foot. "He can learn a little something."

So, at that moment I knew I was trapped. It didn't matter where or when. If Evron wanted me, he would have me. But at least I knew it would be over fast and he would be out of there.

It was then I knew that Evron wasn't what I wanted. Suddenly, getting out of this place seemed more important than ever. I never knew what Mom meant before. But I guessed she must have felt trapped. Just like me.

Getting birth control was easy. Getting away from Evron was hard.

School became the only place I felt safe.

CHAPTER 10

December

I hated the cold. I didn't have a decent jacket. I think I got mine in eighth grade, so I couldn't zip up the front. Mom finally decided I could go get me a new one. It was Saturday. I loved Saturdays when Mom was off work. She would hang out with Benny and me. Evron would stay away. Mom knew he was my boyfriend, but she saw I didn't really want to talk about it. So we didn't.

We rode the bus to the mall, and I felt like a child all over again. Mom and I laughed when people would tell us what a cute girl Benny was. He was wearing my old pink jacket from when I was a baby. Mom would just smile and say thank you. She had no intention of spending money on a new jacket for Benny. As long as he didn't care, then she didn't care.

We headed straight for the marked down items in Sears. I was happy to find a warm jacket for $20. It was originally $99. But the hood was missing. I didn't care. I could always wear one of the wool caps Mom had stuffed in a drawer. I touched the soft blue fleece and was excited to have something so warm. "This is great, Mom!" I looked at her, but she was standing frozen.

I turned to look at Benny pulling up on a coat rack. I wasn't sure why Mom wasn't happy to see Benny trying to stand up. But then I noticed the man standing next to Benny. He was tall and white with the reddest hair I'd ever seen.

"Hi there, little boy." The man was stooping over. He looked slowly up at my mother. "Is this your boy, Jaz?" It had been a while since I had heard anyone call Mom that. Jasmeet was her name, but those closest to her called her Jaz.

Mom nodded and a coolness came into her eyes. "And yours too, Ted."

Ted quickly stood up and walked away from Benny. "Jaz, you know he doesn't look a bit like me."

That's when I got close enough to the man to see his brilliant blue eyes. He was Benny's dad. Mom stepped over to grab Benny. She stared at Ted again. "No, Ted, I guess he doesn't look like you at all."

Ted just nodded and walked away, like we had just been talking about the weather.

"Mom!" I whispered. "But he does look like Benny!"

Mom's shoulders were more relaxed. She looked at me and I could see she was still upset. She tried to push away her feelings and just state the facts. "I know, baby. It's just that he knows Benny is his, but he doesn't care."

"Why don't you do one of those tests?" I said. I thought maybe we could prove it. Maybe that would solve everything. "You know, the one with the DNA match thing."

Mom just shook her head. "I can't." She grabbed my jacket and headed to the cash register.

"Why?"

She handed some money to a lady with lips as red as blood. Then she looked at me. "Because it would make him so mad that I would lose my job. I still work for him and I need that job! Besides, it costs too much."

I just nodded. I knew Mom was stuck. I understood stuck.

CHAPTER 11

Mrs. Grady

Where have you been?" Mrs. Grady didn't sound like her sweet self. I could barely look up at her. My head felt so heavy. She was so close I could taste the smoke from her breath. When I didn't answer, she touched me. The teacher took my arm and squeezed it. I couldn't believe it. My anger finally got me to look at her.

"Don't touch me!" I looked right into her face. The gray stood out along the edge of her hair and down her messy part. It screamed that it needed more red dye.

She took her hand away, but her voice was still firm. "Dani, you have missed three days this week. Last week you missed two. And now you're sleeping. I hear you're sleeping in all of your classes. What's going on?" She pulled a chair up next to me and I could tell she wasn't going anywhere.

I looked at the clock and then at the empty room. I realized that I must have fallen asleep. Everyone else was at lunch. My new coat was so soft and warm. It called for me to just sleep. To rest. To feel at peace.

"Why do you care?" I said as I put my head back on to the desk.

Something changed in her voice. "Because I do. You're one of my best students. You're so close to graduating." She paused. I could feel her touch my arm again. But she was gentle, so I let her. I couldn't figure Mrs. Grady out. She had always been nice. But this year she seemed more into my business than ever.

I lifted my head and tried to smile, but

it was not quite there. "I just got stuff going on at home." I stood up and gathered all my things. I knew Ruth would be waiting for me in front of my locker. But that wasn't fun anymore either. Seeing Ruth meant seeing Evron.

"Is there anything I can do?" Mrs. Grady walked me to the door. She grabbed a large envelope from her desk and handed it to me. "Dani?"

"What's this?" I started to look inside the envelope.

"It's all your missed work." She looked at me again with a look I did not understand. "You've got to make this up. Get it all in to your teachers by the end of next week and you should be able to keep a passing grade."

I felt something stir inside me. I wanted to cry. I wanted to say thank you. I knew I could do this while I watched Benny. I suddenly felt like I could pull this off after all.

But all I could do was look at Mrs. Grady and nod.

When I got to my locker Ruth looked ticked. "What took you so long?"

I opened my locker and started pulling out books. "I fell asleep."

"Oh," said Ruth like it was no big deal. "Don't worry. I do that all the time." She saw my large envelope and grabbed it from me. "What's this?"

"Give it back!" I sounded a little angrier than I should have. It just made Ruth rip into the envelope spilling the papers all over the hall floor. I quickly fell to my knees and started picking the papers up. "Why'd you do that?" I was about to cry.

"What?" Ruth shoved a paper with her foot. "Is this all homework? You got a bunch of homework and you're acting like it's money." I looked up at her and for the first time I really saw that Ruth didn't get it. She didn't get me.

When I had the last piece, I carefully placed them in the back of my history book. I barely whispered, "It's important to me."

"You really think school matters." Ruth got in close. Her breath stunk. "I tell you what matters. You keep Evron and he'll take care of you. And if you're really smart you let him get you pregnant. Then he'll take good care of you and the baby. And if he don't then you can get money from the state for every baby you have."

"What?" I couldn't believe my best friend had just said the stupidest thing I'd ever heard. "Do you really believe that?"

"Yeah! That's what my momma did!" She looked at me and had a mean look. "It's what your momma did."

"It is *not*!" I screamed. "She loved my father and Benny's dad. She's trying to work hard to give us what we need. She says school matters ..." I took a breath.

"Oh, Miss Know-It-All, is that why she's keeping you at home lately with Benny?" Ruth turned to walk away.

I yelled at her again. "You're wrong about your own momma. Your momma works so hard. She's never home! That doesn't sound like being taken care of."

She stopped. Ruth turned one more time. The look was hard and dark. "So, you enjoying Evron? He comes home telling us all what a fine fat ride he got. Then he takes off to get him a real woman."

She was gone. I just held on to my book as I sat on the floor in the middle of the hall. I was alone. Really alone. Tears rolled down my face and I could barely make out Mrs. Grady running to me.

I felt like crap for the rest of the day, but Mrs. Grady told me to stick it out and not let Ruth determine my future. If I went home she would have won. Mrs. Grady was right.

CHAPTER 12

Meat

I left my phone turned off. Evron's texting made me want to puke. I found myself afraid to hang out at home. I didn't want to face Ruth or Evron, so every time Mom needed something done I would beg her to let me take Benny and get out. At first she said she didn't want me walking the streets, but I just told her she was being stupid and that I could help out more.

Christmas was in a week and she wanted some good meat for the 25th of December. She wanted me to check if there were any specials. I was hoping the steaks were on special, but a pork roast would be okay too.

It had been a while since I'd been to the Market Place. It was a bigger store than the Quick Mart on the corner where I picked up most of our bread and milk. I looked forward to seeing the huge amount of food. There was a flower section too. I liked to walk by it and breathe in the sweet smells. I would barely touch a rose, knowing I would waste money if I brought one home.

Benny and I enjoyed the twenty minute bus ride. He would pull himself up and stand with his hands wide open against the windows. I would hold his back so he wouldn't fall. Benny made me smile. Not much made me smile anymore. So I found myself more and more asking Mom if Benny could sleep in my room. He made me feel safe. He gave me peace.

The bus drive went by quickly. We soon got off the bus and headed for the Market Place. We crossed the busy parking lot and went into the building. I found myself laughing at the noise from people on phones. They were running through the store like they were the only people there. After we slowly walked past the flower section, we headed for the meat.

I was looking at the steak behind the glass.

"Hey, Dani. You need help?" I was surprised to see Keon looking at me. His hairnet would have made me laugh if he hadn't been Evron's brother. I just stared and was angry that I had forgotten that Keon worked the meat department. When I didn't say anything he tried to smile. "I thought you had a brother not a sister." He pointed at Benny.

I tried to smile. "Oh, it's my old pink jacket. Benny doesn't care, so Mom and I get a kick out of everyone thinking he's a girl."

"You're crazy!" Keon tried to tease. But his eyes were hiding something. "So what you looking for?"

I looked back at the steak. "Oh. We were looking at your deals on meat." I pointed at the steak.

Then with the same voice, like it was a joke, he said, "I thought you were getting all the meat you needed."

My heart suddenly raced. I felt the urge to puke, and I know I must have looked pale. "What?" I barely whispered.

He just looked at me. Then he suddenly looked away. "You know."

I turned and grabbed Benny and started running down the aisle. I left my shopping cart. I left the steak I wanted. I couldn't breathe.

Benny started crying and I could feel my own tears flow. I didn't stop until I was at the bus stop. I sat down on the bench and just wept. People walking by stared, but they didn't care. I was nobody to them. I was beginning to think I was nobody to anyone.

After twenty minutes of waiting I heard, "I'm sorry." I looked around to find Keon standing with a small plastic bag in his hand. I just looked away. I didn't care that I had snot running out my nose. I wasn't going to wipe it on my jacket.

He sat down next to me. "Here." He handed me a paper towel. It was rough, but it took care of the snot. I still didn't say anything. "I didn't mean to hurt you." He paused. "No, I guess I did mean to hurt you."

I barely spoke, "Why?"

"'Cause, you're better than that," he said as we both kept looking across the street.

"What?" I still didn't get him.

"You're better than sleeping with Ev-ron." He got it out. "I thought you wouldn't stoop so low as to sleep with a loser."

I turned my head to finally look at Keon. His hairnet was gone, but he was still wearing his white butcher jacket. "You really think a lot of your brother."

"He doesn't do anything but hang out and sleep around." Keon said it as a matter of fact.

"That's what I heard," I said.

He looked at me. "So do you get a lot out of it?"

"Evron?" I asked.

"Yeah."

I swallowed hard as tears began to flow. "I hate it. I hate him."

Keon's eyes changed. I could see a flash of anger. "What?" He swallowed. "You don't want Evron?"

I shook my head. "I thought I did. But …," I couldn't believe I was telling Keon what I hadn't told anyone. "He makes me feel ugly. I know he's using me and that he has other girls." Tears just flowed again. "He just takes what he wants."

There was silence. Finally Keon handed me the small plastic bag. "Here. I think this is what you really wanted." I looked inside. There were three beautiful steaks. "Here's some really good meat." He made me smile.

"This is really too many. I only needed two. How much do I owe you?" I reached into my coat to get my money.

He touched my arm. "Nothing." He smiled at me. "Consider it an apology."

I didn't know what to say. I just looked at him. I frowned and finally said, "No strings attached?"

His eyes got really big. I could see he was trying not to get angry. He stared at me hard. "I am not my brother!"

I nodded slowly. "Okay then." I closed the bag. "Thank you."

We sat in silence again. By now an

old lady had started a line. Only two other people were there, but they still stood behind her. I finally saw the bus coming and I stood up. Benny had fallen asleep on my shoulder. Keon stood up with me but did not get in line for the bus.

"I got to head back to work," he said as he looked at me in a sad sort of way. "You okay going home alone?"

"Yeah, I'm good." I turned when I felt his hand on my arm again.

I looked at him as he whispered, "You know you can tell Evron to back off."

I shook my head. "I don't know how. I'm so afraid he'll get mad. And Ruth, she's already mad at me." I tried to turn to get on bus, but his grip tightened.

"Dani, listen to me." I could see something in his eyes that made my stomach turn again. But, in a good way. "Evron will back off. You just got to give him a reason to." He paused, then he said with a fire in his eyes, "Or I will!"

I left Keon standing at the bus stop. I could feel the weight of the meat in my hand. Somehow the beautiful cuts of steak made me feel lighter than I had in a long time.

CHAPTER 13

Christmas

I loved our little tree. I made it in kindergarten out of green pipe cleaners. It was small, but it was Christmas. Mom always said that this way she could spend money on us and not a tree. I thought it sounded good at the time. So the pipe cleaner tree would be pulled out of a bottom drawer and reshaped every year.

Mom said she had to take off for work at ten, so we quickly opened our gifts. Benny got my old Elmo doll that mom wrapped up. At first Benny loved the paper more than the little red character. But it wasn't long before he was chewing on Elmo's hand. Mom and I just smiled.

I loved the new bag mom got me. I could use it like a book bag or a large purse. Then Mom laughed when she saw me find new socks and underwear shoved in the bottom of it.

"What's this?" Mom was surprised when I handed her a small box.

"It's for you." I smiled as Mom opened the small box. A sweet necklace soon hung around her neck as she looked in the mirror. Then she asked me. "Where'd you get the money to pay for this?"

"It wasn't much, Mom." I smiled. "I used the money I had for the steaks." I told her how Keon had given us the steaks after being a jerk to me. She looked a little confused. But she was happy to see the small silver chain shine against her dark skin.

She kissed me and said she'd be back around seven to enjoy the steaks. With her gone I turned on the TV to watch some holiday specials.

"Dani!" The knock at the door was strong.

Evron's voice made me want to run and lock myself in the bathroom. I was mad that I hadn't locked the door after Mom left. I quickly stood up and ran to the door to see if I could lock it before he tried to open it. My heart raced as I started to turn the lock. Just as the lock clicked, I slid to the floor shaking.

Then the pounding started. "Dani! I know you're in there. I heard you! Let me in, baby. I need you." I stayed quiet. "*Dani! Let me in!*" The pounding was harder. "*You better let me in!*"

"Shut up!" A neighbor yelled. "Or I'll call the police!"

Evron took one last whack at my door. "You can't hide from me, Dani!" Then he was gone.

I didn't leave the apartment. When Mom came home I tried to pretend that I was happy when we ate our amazing steaks. But I was pretending.

CHAPTER 14

January

Dani, I need you to watch Benny again today." Mom tried to sound matter of fact, but I could hear the strain in her voice.

I slowly put my school books down on the kitchen table. "Again?" I sat down feeling like I had no control. It didn't matter how hard I worked at school, I was always behind. I looked at Mom but she looked bad. She hadn't fixed her hair and pieces stuck out like wire. Tears started to fall. "Mom? What is it?"

She sat down at the table with me. "I'm so sorry, baby. I need you to watch Benny until I find another sitter."

"What?" I was staring hard.

"Mrs. Parks said she couldn't watch Benny anymore. Her husband took on a night shift, so he needs to sleep during the day. They can't have a baby keeping him up." Mom tried to stop crying. Her voice was calm, but tears just flowed.

"Mom, I'm so close to finishing school," I whispered. I was begging.

She suddenly stood up. She wiped her face. She smoothed out her hair. "I know." She looked almost mad. "I can't help it, Dani. It's where we are."

It was no use talking back. I just dropped my face on to my history book. I tried to cover my head so Mom wouldn't see me cry. I could hear her getting her purse and kissing Benny. Then I felt her kiss my head. "I'll keep looking."

I didn't answer.

CHAPTER 15

The Letter

Getting mail just didn't happen. So when a letter arrived, I was really surprised. As soon as I opened it, I wished the letter had never come. It was from my school. I was not going to get credit due to too many absences. The letter then asked us to come in for a meeting to look at my options. It gave a time and date for the meeting. I realized the letter must have been in our mailbox for a few days because the date was that afternoon.

I had nothing better to do, so I got Benny dressed and walked to school with a baby on my arm. It felt so weird going into the building. I had not set foot in there for two weeks. I was happy the halls were empty as I headed for the counselor's office. It was funny to see the look on the face of the young blond lady at the first desk. It was like she didn't expect me. She even said, "Oh, you came? We weren't expecting you."

At first I thought I had done something wrong, so I pulled out my letter. "But the date and time says I should be here now."

I saw the lady push a blond strand of hair behind her ear as she turned red. She picked up the phone. "Let me see if I can find someone to talk to you."

I suddenly got it. She didn't expect me because they never really thought I would show up. They thought I was some loser trying to get out of school. I felt my cheeks getting warm. I bit my lower lip to keep myself from crying.

The lady finally got off the phone and

pointed to a bench. "If you wait over there, someone will be with you in a little while. Mr. Smith is in a meeting." She tried to turn and get back to work.

I slowly moved to the hard wooden bench. I shifted Benny to my other hip before I turned to face her again. "Let me get this straight. You called me in for this meeting and the man is in a different meeting?" I tried not to be mean, but I wasn't doing a good job.

"Now, honey, it's no reason to get mad." She was turning red herself.

"Don't you honey me!" I turned and sat down. I looked at the wall so I wouldn't have to see the woman's face. I would wait. I didn't care if Benny cried. When his diaper needed changing, I took my time. I changed him right there on the bench. Then I dumped his dirty diaper in the trash can nearest to her desk. The woman started to say something but stopped when she saw my face. I took my time. I didn't say another word. I waited.

An hour later Mr. Smith came into the office and looked at me. He smiled like I should be happy to see him. I didn't smile back. I couldn't tell if he was old or just looked it. He had dark circles under his eyes that made his white skin look really pale and sick. He was sweating and wiped his head on his sleeve. "Ms. Garcia?" I just nodded. He walked toward a closed door, and he turned to glance at me. "Please come into my office."

I followed him and sat down in an old leather chair. The room was stuffy. He sat at his desk and folded his hands. I wasn't sure if he wanted to talk first. He just looked at Benny as if I'd pulled him out of a hat. Mr. Smith finally spoke, "How can I help you?" I handed him the letter. He took a moment to look at it. "Oh, I am pleased you came in," he lied.

"Looks like you didn't think I would come," I finally said.

He tried to smile. "Oh, we just send out so many of these letters, and we don't usually get a response this quickly. People call and set up a different time. Or," he paused for a moment, "they just don't bother to come back." He looked at Benny and then at me. "Considering you have a child, I am surprised you …"

"What?" I was shocked. "Benny's my brother!" I could feel my cheeks burning. "You are assuming a lot about me, mister. Tell me what my options are and I'll get out of here." I was holding back tears, "Unless you *want* to add me to your drop-out list."

Mr. Smith's eyes softened. He cleared his throat. "I am sorry. Please don't let my stupidity make you stop coming." He handed me a tissue. "Please tell me why you have so many absences."

I took the tissue and I told him we were having baby-sitting issues. He nodded and listened. I told him how my teachers had been giving me work, but it was getting harder to keep up. "So the letter said I had another option. What is it?"

Mr. Smith reached into a stack and pulled out a form. "It sounds like you would be perfect for our partnership with West Side Community College." He handed me a paper with teenage faces smiling on it. "They offer night classes every weeknight. You can get started to-night. You can pick up the needed credits. They still count as high school credits, so you can graduate on time. And if you do well, you could begin some college classes in July."

My head was suddenly spinning. College? "But we don't have money to pay." He handed me another form.

"Have your mother fill this out. The

night classes are paid for through a drop-out prevention grant. To get into their college on a scholarship in July, you will have to do well this semester." He looked at me and really smiled this time. "Show them you're serious. Just like you showed me."

CHAPTER 16
Hope

Hope is a strong word. But that's what I felt. I couldn't believe I actually had options. Then I felt stupid for not having asked anyone. I guess it's easier to think there is no way out than to keep looking until you find something. Mom was all for it, and I couldn't wait.

Leaving Mom and Benny behind, I hopped on the bus that took me one stop past the Market Place. I smiled as I watched the store pass by, remembering Keon's words. I had managed to keep Evron away. And Ruth. She hadn't tried to talk to me. I was finding that more time away made me feel I could live without her friendship. But it still hurt.

The building for night classes was only a block away from the bus stop. There were a lot of people. I found the classroom. As I looked around the room, I saw more than just teens. I couldn't believe how many different types of people were there. Black, white, Hispanic, Asian, and some I couldn't tell. They looked so different from my high school class. I finally figured out what was different about them. They were serious. They wanted to learn.

I found a seat in the back next to people who were paying no attention to me. They were getting out their books and waiting for the teacher to speak.

I opened up my notebook. I took out my pen. I felt something rise inside me that left me feeling strong. I was taking back my life. I was going to make it.

CHAPTER 17

February

I let down my guard. I guess that's the best way to describe it. I was used to the bus trip and felt safe with my new routine. It seemed great to be able to sleep in and spend most of the day watching Benny while getting my homework done. Around six, Mom would run into the house and kiss me as I walked out the door for class. As far as I could tell, I was an A student.

It was nine when I got off the bus that night. I was heading straight for our apartment building when I heard a car pull up next to me. "Hey, Dani. What you doing out so late?" Evron's voice sounded different. He was drunk or high. I couldn't tell which, but I wasn't going to ask.

"School!" I tried to sound calm, but my voice cracked. "Got to go!" I picked up speed and started to run. I heard the car door slam, and Evron was on me as I touched the cold front door. He jerked me back twice before I let go of the handle.

My arm hurt. My heart pounded. I screamed and begged. He just pulled me to his car. I felt I couldn't breathe. My head hit a pile of small boxes. But I didn't care what was in his car. I wanted out.

Five minutes later I was on the side of the street. My jacket was ripped, my sweet jacket. I don't know how long I lay there. I was cold. I was alone. I could taste blood on my lips. I was slow to feel my pants lying next to me on the sidewalk. I finally tried to cover myself as I heard the bus pull up again.

Rushing footsteps stopped beside me. I couldn't tell who it was. But the arms were strong and gentle. All I heard was, "Dani! Oh my God!" Then I blacked out.

CHAPTER 18

Broken Pieces

Sounds and sights all became a blur. All I knew was that there were lots of people talking and just as many touching me. I remember trying to push hands away. All I heard were words, but not sentences. Examine. Kit. Hair. Blood.

The hospital bed was soft. I felt so far away. I didn't want to come back, but I finally woke to the sound of my own scream. "Dani, baby. Are you okay?" Mom was crying and her touch finally pulled me back to this world.

"Evron hurt me." I sounded like a three year old. I felt like a three year old. All I wanted was to be held.

Mom climbed up on the bed with me and pulled me close. "I know, baby. The police are here and want to talk to you. But they'll wait until you're ready."

I couldn't seem to push away the fog from my brain. I didn't understand. How could she know? I tried to speak, but I could only close my eyes. A few hours later, I woke again. This time I could see the room. Mom was still next to me, and I could hear Benny giggle. I tried to focus my eyes on the wonderful sound. If Mom was with me, then who was holding Benny? The giggle was stronger this time, and I was able to completely focus. Keon was smiling at Benny as he kept lifting him up and down into the air.

"Keon?" I was confused.

The tall, dark figure suddenly came over to me. His smile was gone and the same look appeared that I saw that night at the bus stop. I could see he was angry. "Hi, Dani."

"Keon found you, baby." Mom's voice was weak. "He called the police and gave them all the info they needed."

I looked at him, but I had no smile to give. "Thank you, Keon."

He reached out to touch my hand but stopped as I pulled away. His eyes met mine and he could see my fear. He placed Benny on the bed and let him crawl up to me. Keon touched the top of Benny's head and turned to leave. But just before he walked out the door, he looked at me and said, "Dani, I will never let this happen to you again."

I just looked at Mom and cried. How could Keon make sure it didn't happen again? How could I ever leave my apartment again? How could I ever pick up the broken pieces?

CHAPTER 19
Questions

"Are you sure you're ready?" Mom looked at me as I sat up in the hospital bed. A white man dressed in a suit stood next to me with a pad of paper. I nodded. I tried not to stare at his shiny bald spot. He was trying to hide it with some hair, but it wasn't working.

The balding man faked a smile. "Are you sure?" His voice showed that he was ready to talk, even if I wasn't. He pointed at a short, fat black man in a police uniform. His head was shaved. *He* wasn't trying to hide *anything*. The white man's voice pulled me back. "I'm Detective Mills and this Officer Jones. We are here to ask you a few questions."

I could feel my heart beat. I started to breathe hard. "About what?"

The two men looked at each other and Mills put down his pen. He sighed, "About last night."

"Oh." I looked at Mom. I wished she could answer for me, but she couldn't. She squeezed my hand. I swallowed. "Evron attacked me."

Mills picked up his pen. "Evron Smith?"

"Yes."

He looked at his pad of paper as he asked the next question. "What happened exactly?" There was a long pause and he finally looked up. I was staring at him and tears started to spill down my cheeks. He looked at Mom. "Ma'am, we can come back later."

"No," I yelled a little too loud. I didn't

want to wait. I wanted them to help me now. "I was coming home from night school and Evron pulled me into his car."

"Did you want to get into the car?" Mills asked.

I frowned. "What? No! He pulled me and forced me and …" I told them. Every last bit of it. It didn't take long, but it felt like forever. When it was over I covered my head with my covers. I didn't want them to see my silent scream.

I could barely hear Mills say, "Thank you, Dani."

I calmed myself to hear Mom ask, "What next?"

Mills answered, "We'll find Evron Smith and question him. The hospital will send us the rape kit, and we'll begin to build a case. We need Dani's phone records and some of her clothes. "

"You won't arrest him?" Mom's voice was shaking.

"Oh yes we will." Mills paused. "But …"

I stayed under the covers as I heard Mom's voice get loud. "But what?"

"He might be able to post bail." He paused for a moment. "It all depends on if he has the cash to pay it."

I peeked out from my covers. I was feeling a little hope rise. I whispered, "Mom, they don't have any money. They won't be able to pay."

Mom reached over and touched my head. "I know, baby." Then she turned back to Mills. Her voice was serious again. "What if he does post bail? How long before trial? Before he goes to jail?"

Mills shook his head. He knew Mom wouldn't like his answer. "It could be months, maybe even a year."

"*Months? A year?*" Mom yelled. I watched Mom stand to face the men. Officer Jones stepped in and touched Mom's arm. "Don't touch me!" She glared at Jones.

"Ma'am." Mills was still calm. "Trust me. If he posts bail, which is a slim chance, it is not likely that he will hurt Dani again. He has no prior arrests."

Mom stared hard. "But you don't know that!"

"No." Mills held Mom's stare. "We don't know that he won't hurt her again."

Mom sat back down and took my hand again. "But what about Dani?"

Mills reached in his pocket and handed Mom a card. "Here's the number of a counselor that works with the police and handles rape cases. Please call her. She can guide Dani."

Guide me? Whatever that meant. I wasn't about to call anyone. I was done talking about it. I wasn't ever going to tell my story again.

CHAPTER 20

Slim Chance

We had come home earlier that day. Mom was getting ready to make herself some noodles. I didn't want to eat. I was too tired. I was heading to bed when the phone rang. Mom picked it up and listened for a minute before she smiled at me and whispered, "It's Detective Mills. They picked up Evron."

She turned her head to hear what else Mills had to say. I felt some relief flow through my body. I was tired. Real tired. But now I could sleep. First I wanted to hear what Mills had to say. I stopped heading for my bedroom. I decided to sit on the couch. I carefully sat down and waited.

The phone call went on for a while. Longer than I thought it should. Mom finally said, "You're kidding me! How did he get the money?" My body tightened again. I kept waiting for there to be good news again. But Mom soon ended the call with, "Thank you, Detective Mills. We'll be waiting to hear from you. Bye." She hung up and looked at me.

"What?" I asked. But I already understood what Mills had told Mom before she started to explain. But I listened anyway, just in case I was wrong. I wasn't.

"Mills told me they did pick up Evron. They found him sleeping at home. Evron said he didn't know what the police were talking about. Of course the results from the rape kit made him angry, and he blamed you for the whole thing." Mom paused. She walked over to the sink and let the water run. "They pressed charges." She put a pot under the tap and filled it half way.

I got up off the couch and followed her. "And?" Why didn't she get to the point?

She walked to the stove and put the pot on the top. Turning on a burner, she looked at me. "He made bail."

"What?" I was upset. "How much was it?"

"Twenty-five hundred dollars." Mom said it as she pulled the noodles out from behind a neatly stacked pile of cans and cereal.

"Who paid it?" I was not sure how Evron's family could come up with the money that fast.

Mom looked at me. She was frowning. "He paid it. With cash."

"What?" I leaned against the wall. "How's that possible?"

Mom shook her head. "That's what I want to know." Mom pointed at the phone. "That's what the police want to know."

CHAPTER 21

Fear

I have never felt fear like I did that first week back home. I didn't want to leave the apartment. I didn't want to go to school. Evron was not in jail. He paid his own bail. He was out. He was living only a few floors above me.

Mom called the police hoping they could give her some direction on how to deal with me. The police reminded us that it took time to go to trial. We would have to be patient. Patient? You try being patient while having that kind of fear. I was so scared. As far as I was concerned, it would be okay if I didn't leave our apartment until the trial was over. Talk about being frozen in time. I cried all day long. I would look at my school books and I would cry. I would look in the mirror and I would cry. I would look at my ripped jacket and I would cry.

After a week of this, Mom entered my room. "Enough!" she said as she pulled the covers off of me. I was still in bed at five in the afternoon. Mrs. Carson had agreed to watch Benny for a week while I got better. Whatever better meant. Mom was taking charge. "You are going to school tonight."

Fear made my chest feel so tight that I screamed, "No, I can't!" I pulled the covers back up and cried.

Mom was not gentle. "Yes, you can! You will get your life back! The sooner, the better. Don't you dare let Evron steal it away."

"He already did," I said as I looked at

Mom. She was strong and beautiful. Her hair was up, so you could see her strong cheek bones. She wearing the necklace I gave her for Christmas. I reached up and touched the sliver chain. I felt like I was trying to reach for something. I wanted that happy moment back. I wanted Mom smiling at me. I wanted to be sitting in front of the handmade Christmas tree again. The memory seemed a lifetime ago.

Her eyes softened just a little. "Baby, he's going to pay a price. When and how, I don't know. But you *will* fight."

I sat up and tried to wipe away the tears. Snot stuck to my sheet. "How?"

She threw some jeans and a shirt on my bed. "By getting dressed and getting to class."

"Mom, I'm just so scared!" I slowly reached for the shirt.

Mom put both her hands on her hips. "We have a plan." She smiled and all her teeth showed. I felt a little bit of hope rise from somewhere inside. "I'll walk you to the bus stop. And when you are on the way home, Keon will get on the bus in front of the Market Place. He'll make sure you get home."

"But Keon's shift isn't over." I was confused.

"He's worked it out so he can go in earlier and leave earlier." She smiled again. She reached into the pocket at the back of her jeans. "And here." She threw a new phone at me with a new number. "Only Keon and I have your new number. So please think about who you give it to."

"Oh." I held the phone in my hands like a strange object I had never seen before. It seemed like a plan that might work. I wasn't sure why Keon would do this for me. But right then it really didn't matter why; I just needed someone to make me feel safe.

CHAPTER 22
Stepping Back into Life

I never pictured myself one of those people who keep looking over their shoulder. But I was. Every noise made me jump. Sitting on the bus alone, I watched every person get on and off. I looked behind me every minute. By the time the bus stopped for me, I was sweating. But I didn't take off my jacket.

I ran from the bus stop to the classroom. By the time I sat down, I was breathing so hard that people stared. I got up and ran to the bathroom and cried. I wanted to go home. But I couldn't get on the bus yet because then Keon wouldn't be with me. Then I got scared alone in the bathroom and ran back to the classroom. I tried to sit in the back, so people wouldn't see my face. Or my ripped jacket. Mom repaired it because I needed it. But it looked like a huge scar that everyone could see.

"Are you okay?" A sweet voice whispered with a slight accent. I looked to my left and saw a girl who was Latino.

"I'm fine!" I lied.

"No, you're not!" She shook her head and cussed in Spanish. Of course those were the only Spanish words I knew.

I looked at her. Her dark hair with a blond stripe down the side was in a tight pony tail. I could see she had her nose pierced. I tried to smile. "You're right. I'm not okay." She looked at me as if I would tell her more. But I just shook my head. "I just can't talk about it right now."

She whispered, "Don't worry about it." She smiled. "I'm Eva."

"Dani Garcia." I smiled. "But I don't speak Spanish."

Eva laughed and then we both turned to listen to the teacher. Something about Eva made me relax. It felt good to feel relaxed for a change.

After class I stood at the door of the building. The bus stop was only around the corner, but it was dark. Really dark. The streetlights didn't make me feel any better. I had done this so many times. But today the walk seemed hard. I started to shake.

"Dani?" Eva was standing next to me. "What's wrong?"

I looked at her and tried to wipe away the tear that was starting to fall. "Oh, hi Eva." I paused as I watched her look at me really funny. Then I asked, "Could you walk me to the bus stop?"

She lifted her eyebrows. "Sure." We

started toward the bus stop. For a few minutes she was quiet, but finally she said, "It must have been bad." She wasn't asking me anything. It was just a statement.

I looked at her for just a minute and was not sure why she said that. "What do you mean?"

She stopped and looked right at me. "Look, Dani. I know you were attacked." She jerked her head toward the school. "We all do." The look of horror on my face made her come in closer. "Don't worry. We all are there for you. The teacher found out why you missed last week and told us."

"He shouldn't have!" I was angry. I started to walk again. I walked fast.

"Bull!" Eva quickly caught up. "We should know! We should watch out for you. We have to stick together."

I stopped again and looked at her. I hated it. But something about what she said was right. I guessed Mom probably told the teacher. I smiled for a minute thinking Mom was making sure strangers would watch out for her baby. "You're right, Eva." I smiled at her. "I don't know you, but I do need you."

"I know." Eva smiled back. She grabbed my arm and turned me around. "Now let's go get you on that bus."

CHAPTER 23

Bus Angel

It was only a ten minute ride before I saw the tall, dark figure get on the bus. Keon walked right up to me and sat down with his leg touching mine. I pulled my leg away. He just smiled and said, "I hope your first day back was good."

"Not really. Well, sort of," I said looking straight ahead.

"Which is it?" he asked. He looked straight ahead too.

"I was afraid. It was bad. But I met someone." I smiled to myself.

There was a pause. Keon shifted a moment and then asked, "You met someone?"

He turned his head toward me for just a minute before turning away again. I suddenly laughed. I hadn't laughed in a long time. Keon was acting like a shy ten-year-old. He didn't laugh. "What's so funny?"

"You!" I gently shoved his shoulder. "I met a girl, stupid! She's a new friend."

"Oh." He sighed. He turned toward me again. I knew he was trying to look at me. I couldn't help but try to look back. It was dark, but suddenly the lights from outside lit up Keon's cheek. Then the moment was gone.

I gasped. "What's wrong with your cheek? It looks swollen."

Keon paused for only a moment. He leaned down, so only I could hear. He spoke slowly. "I beat the crap out of Evron. I told him if he touched you again I would kill him. Of course he got some hits in too." I could feel him try to look at me again. The city lights lit up the bus again.

For only a moment. I got a glimpse of his eyes. I could see for just a moment that his eyes held something new. Something I had never known from any man. I mattered. I really mattered.

CHAPTER 24

March

I kept hoping the fear would go away. But it didn't. I seemed to be able to manage getting to school and back. But I never left the apartment any other time of the day.

I told myself that this was good. I had more time to work on my school work, and it was paying off. I smiled at every A I brought home. I didn't do much smiling though, except with Benny and Keon. I would smile when Benny would yell my name—Ni Ni—as he ran into my arms.

I would also feel a small smile sneak up as Keon sat next to me on the bus. Or when he'd text me to just say hi and tell

me what he was doing. But the rest of
the time I felt a deep empty hole that just
seemed to get bigger as the days went on.
I couldn't get rid of the thought that Evron
slept only three floors above us.

CHAPTER 25

The Visitor

The knock on the door sent fear through my body. I stood still. The door was locked and the stove clock read four p.m. Mom wasn't supposed to be home yet. Benny was taking a nap on Mom's bed. It was so quiet. I just stood there as the knocking continued. A few minutes passed and I realized the knock had not turned into pounding. I slowly walked toward the door with my heart beating so hard I thought I might pass out.

"Who is it?" I asked with my face touching the cold chain that kept me safe.

"It's Mrs. Grady, dear." The sound of my teacher's voice melted away all my fears. I quickly unlocked the door and saw the little old woman look at me with arms wide open. "Come here, sweetie." I found myself embraced by the smell of cigarettes. I loved it. It was Mrs. Grady. I was safe with Mrs. Grady.

She walked into the little apartment without looking at the empty pizza box from two weeks ago sitting on the kitchen floor next to a very full trash can. She didn't care that she had to step over Benny's toys. She moved a pile of dirty clothes to the side of the couch as she sat down. She folded her hands in her lap and looked at me.

"I'm sorry about the mess," I said as I grabbed the dirty clothes and threw them into my room.

"What mess?" She smiled. "You should see my place." I knew she was lying, but I loved her for it. I sat down next to her.

"What are you doing here?" I said feeling like there might be something I had done wrong.

"I thought you might need me." She patted my leg quickly and folded her hands again. I didn't say anything as I tried to hold back tears. She looked at me and said, "I am so proud of you. You are doing well in the night school program. I checked, you know." She winked at me, making me smile as I wiped my eyes. "I understand you are a survivor."

I frowned a little. "I don't think I am."

She looked at me with a worried look. "Why not? You have continued to do well in spite of your …" she paused not knowing what to say. I knew she didn't want to call it an accident, since it was no such thing. I knew she didn't want to use the word rape, because it was too hard to swallow. So she just said, "You know." This, of course, seemed to be the best word to use since I *did* know.

"Yeah, I know," I said and took Benny's Elmo in my arms to squeeze. "But I am still so afraid."

Mrs. Grady touched my hand this time, but I didn't pull away. "I understand, but this will take time." We sat for a moment in silence before she added, "Have you met with someone yet?" I looked at her confused. "A rape counselor?" She finally said *the word* quickly, as if it were a curse word that she was not allowed to repeat.

I shook my head. "No, I didn't know I should see one." I felt sort of stupid, like I was letting my teacher know I didn't read the directions to a test.

Surprise and anger flooded the little old lady's eyes. "Nobody at the hospital or the police told you about this?"

I dropped my eyes. "Yes, they did." I got up and walked over to the fridge where Mom had taped the card. I took it and handed it to Mrs. Grady. I spoke before she could say anything. "But I just think it's okay if I don't see her."

She stood up and started pacing, accidently kicking a small ball across the room. "This is not okay!" I had never heard Mrs. Grady raise her voice. But she was angry. "You must speak with someone! I will personally see to it that you see this counselor."

"But I don't want to." I felt the tears fall. "I don't want to talk about it. It's over! It's in the past. I want to move on! I don't want to be afraid anymore!" I found myself standing up and yelling.

Mrs. Grady moved in close and held both of my hands. I had never seen Mrs. Grady cry, but tears flowed. "You must, sweet Dani! You must!"

Just then Benny started to cry. I quickly pulled myself away from Mrs. Grady's hands and ran to get Benny. He hugged me as we came back to Mrs. Grady. Her look had changed. She stared at Benny and moved in close. She hesitated for a moment and then gently touched his chubby legs.

"This is Benny," I said. I was thankful that we could move on to a different topic.

"Oh, he is so beautiful. Look at those blue eyes!" She touched his head and took his little hand in hers. She gently kissed his little fingers as Benny giggled. Suddenly she pulled herself together and became my teacher again. "Well, I better go."

"Thanks for coming, Mrs. Grady." I walked her to the door. "I'll think about what you said."

Mrs. Grady looked at me. "No, Dani. I will make sure you talk to …" She paused and looked at the card. "Mrs. Elpidia. This is not for you to think about." I was shocked at her tone. I didn't dare argue back. She smiled, handed the card to me, and patted my hand once more. "We'll get you through this!"

Then she looked at Benny once more and kissed his little toes. "Bye bye, Benny." Benny giggled as I closed the door. I wasn't sure if I should have been thankful or upset about Mrs. Grady's visit. I just wanted to move on, but there was something about Mrs. Grady that made me think I was missing something. I just couldn't figure it out.

CHAPTER 26

Not Again

Mom's look was familiar. She looked quickly away when our eyes met. She finally said, "I'm sorry, baby."

"What are you talking about, Mom?" I was packing up my school books and getting ready to head to the bus.

"I have to work late three nights a week for the next two months." She started cleaning old plates off the kitchen table. When I didn't answer she tried to explain. "Ted gave me first pick at some overtime while Brit is out recovering from an accident." I just looked at her. "You know, I told you about Brit."

"No you didn't, Mom," I said as calmly as I could. I had never heard of Brit and I didn't care about Brit. "You don't have to take the extra hours."

Mom put the last paper plate in the trash. "Yes, I do. It's a way for me to make more money and show Ted that I can do more. Maybe he'll promote me."

"Mom! Are you really that stupid to think Benny's father wants to promote you?" I knew I shouldn't have said it, but it was out. She slapped me. My mother had never slapped me before. She had spanked me when I was little, but this was different. I don't know if tears flowed from the sting or from the hurt.

"Don't you *ever* talk to me like that again!" Her voice was shaking. She just stood there with shock in her eyes. I knew she was just as shocked about the slap as I was. "Dani, I am trying to do my best."

I whispered, "So am I."

"You can go to school the other two days," she said. As if that were a real option.

"You know that's not enough," I said as I headed for the door. I stopped and stared. I didn't like my mother right then. I saw a woman who didn't keep her promise. I would never finish school. "Well, are you going to walk me to the bus or not? I have at least tonight to pretend I might graduate!"

Mom grabbed Benny and threw their jackets on. We walked to the bus in silence. I guess there was nothing else to be said.

CHAPTER 27

Eva

I pretended everything was normal. I pretended that Mom was going to come home and tell me it was all a mistake. I got off the bus and ran into the classroom hoping that I could pretend my way into reality.

I got out my notes and looked to the front of the class. I tried to hear what the teacher was saying, but it was all just noise. I wasn't even taking notes. Eva noticed.

"What's wrong, girl?" Eva sat next to me, like every night. We always shared notes and helped each other with questions we didn't get right.

"Mom's got to work three nights a week for a few months," I whispered. We were far enough back, and the teacher was loud enough that I wasn't too worried that he might hear.

"What?" Eva shook her head. "That sucks!" We both pretended to listen to the lecture, but I still couldn't hear anything.

"Yeah. I guess I'll figure something out one way or another." I looked down at my notebook and tried to write something down.

Eva leaned in and whispered, "Maybe I can help and give you the notes you miss. Would that help?"

I smiled at Eva. "That might. I don't want to stop coming. But maybe if they see I can keep my grades up, they'll overlook the days I miss."

"Shhh." The girl in front of us had had enough. "Some of us are trying to hear the teacher."

"Sorry," Eva whispered. Then she looked at me again. "It just might work."

"It just might," I whispered. I wrote down my telephone number. Eva was the first person I dared to give my number to. As I handed it to her I whispered, "Thanks, Eva."

I turned to face the teacher. Suddenly the noise turned into words and the words turned into sentences. I could hear what he was saying. I could learn again.

CHAPTER 28

Ruth Who?

Trying to learn through notes ended up being more stressful than I thought it would be. To top off my stress, Mrs. Grady set up a meeting for me to meet a Mrs. Elpidia at her office. I should have been happy that it was early afternoon. The problem was I had to take the bus to her office building. This meant I had to pack up Benny and get on the bus by myself.

I opened the door and looked carefully into the hall. I heard a door slam above me and footsteps, so I quickly closed the door again. But the footsteps passed by my door and headed down the steps. So I opened the door again. This time there was no sound. I grabbed Benny. I quickly ran down the stairs and all the way to the bus stop. The bus was already there, ready to close its doors when we jumped on.

Benny and I sat in the first seat I found. I took a deep breath.

I could feel someone scoot up to sit behind me. "What's the rush?" It was weird to hear Ruth's voice. I looked around. She had her hair in tight corn rows. She was wearing more make-up than ever and seemed to be dressed to party.

"Skipping school?" I asked. I wasn't about to tell her where I was going.

"Nope. Dropped out last month." She sucked air through her teeth. "Got better things to do."

I could only imagine with the way she was dressed. But I played along. I nodded and hoped she would get off the bus before we reached our stop. We sat quietly for a while. Benny tried to reach for her but I kept pushing his arms down.

A few stops before ours, Ruth stood up and I started to breathe again. But suddenly she leaned in and whispered, "I think you should drop the charges against my brother."

I could feel my cheeks burn. But I didn't say anything. Fear began to well up, freezing me in place. Her voice felt like ice. "You know you liked every minute of it. You're just a tease, and it's your fault. You made Evron want you, and now he's gonna pay. You slut!" She turned and jumped off as the bus stopped in front of an apartment building I hadn't noticed before. A young black man with a slick suit on nodded at Ruth. I couldn't see his face. She quickly caught up to him and they headed into the building. She didn't look back at me. She didn't care what I saw or thought.

I wanted to puke. Who was Ruth? She was not the person I grew up with. How could she ever have been my friend? How could she really think that Evron was innocent?

CHAPTER 29

Counseling

I don't remember getting off the bus. But I did. I was in a large waiting room outside several office doors. I looked for Mrs. Elpidia's office and sat down across from it. Benny tore into magazines as I waited. I didn't stop him. There were a couple of other people there, but they didn't care either. They just looked the other way.

Soon I could hear one of the doors open, but I didn't look up.

"Are you okay?" A tall Hispanic lady wearing high heels and red lipstick sat down next to me. When I didn't answer she asked, "Are you Dani Garcia?"

I just nodded and she led me into her office. She pulled out a box of toys and Benny quickly dropped the half-chewed picture of Oprah. "Dani, tell me what's wrong?"

I had never seen a counselor like her before. I guessed they were all like Mr. Smith from school, but I was wrong. Mrs. Elpidia was looking at me as if she really wanted to know. It didn't make sense to me since she didn't know me. I had never seen her before, so why should she care?

"Nothing," I lied. But tears showed my true feelings. Benny fussed a little and climbed into my arms holding a truck.

"Oh." She smiled softly. "Do you cry over nothing a lot?" I just nodded. She kept smiling. "Well, Dani. I can't help you if you don't talk."

I frowned a little and asked, "Talk about what?"

She started to speak, but then stopped.

She leaned back in her chair and took a deep breath. "Whatever you need to talk about." The beautiful, slick woman used her best counseling tone. It was like loud music pounding in my head. I wanted to turn it off. I didn't want to listen to someone who was trying to fake caring about me.

"I don't need to talk about anything," I said and looked at Benny who was starting to fall asleep in my arms. I took the truck out of his hands and put it on the chair next to me. Mrs. Elpidia didn't say anything. She looked at me and Benny. I started to feel weird about the quiet. I finally couldn't take it anymore. "Look! I am here because Mrs. Grady said I should come. I trust her and …"

"You don't trust me." She said it as a matter of fact. But it still hit me like a ton of bricks. She was right. I didn't trust her. I hardly trusted anyone.

I nodded and didn't say anything. I didn't want to be rude. It just happened.

She sat down in the chair next to me. I could smell her perfume. It was okay, I guess. I wasn't one for wearing perfume. I realized at that moment that I wasn't wearing make-up or even a clean shirt. I was not looking my best. I didn't want to look at this perfect woman in front of me. What did she know about how I felt?

"Time will heal." She finally said. She touched Benny's sleeping face. His nose had snot crusted in the corners. His hair was pressed flat against his cheek where spit had glued it to his skin. She still touched him.

"What do you know?" I tried to soften my question without being rude, but it was hard. I really didn't want to cry, but my throat was hurting bad. I knew the floodgates were about to open.

Mrs. Elpidia looked straight into my

eyes. I could see she was holding back her own tears. I could barely hear her whisper, "Because I was you not long ago." I just stared. She continued to look straight at me, "Dani, you are not the only woman to be raped. You are not alone."

CHAPTER 30

Detective Mills

Dani has told you everything." Mom was sitting next to me on the couch. Detective Mills was sitting in the only other chair in the room. We had pushed most of the mess into the bedroom before we opened the door for him. But Mills still handed us Elmo from his chair before he sat down.

"I understand that, Mrs. Garcia," Mills was calm. "But we have to go over the events again to make sure she has not missed anything." He looked at me and didn't smile. He was serious. "There could be one thing you are missing, Dani."

"But didn't you tell us that the rape

case had enough evidence?" Mom questioned Mills as he pressed down his few strands of hair to the top of his head.

"Yes, Mrs. Garcia," Mills started.

"Call me Jasmeet." Mom smiled, trying to be nice. Mills looked awkwardly at her. She explained, "If we are going to keep seeing this much of each other, I'd prefer you to use my name. Not my ex-husband's. I kept the last name for my daughter's sake. Most people call me Jasmeet."

With a little relief Mills continued, "Well, Jasmeet. You are right, but we are looking for any other evidence that might help us otherwise."

"Otherwise?" I was confused. "With what?"

Detective Mills looked around like he was making sure no one else was there. He finally said, "We have found other evidence on Evron Smith's phone that makes us believe he may be charged with other crimes. The fact that he paid the bail with cash makes us believe we may be on to something."

"What other crimes?" Mom asked.

Mills shook his head, "I'm sorry, Jasmeet." He said her name like he was practicing it. "We can't tell you that."

"Are the crimes worse than what my daughter has been through?" Mom was using her best calm voice. But her anger was starting to show.

Mills looked straight at Mom. He was serious. His voice was gentle. "No, Jasmeet, not more serious than what happened to Dani." Mom calmed down some. I could tell she was starting to trust this man. He continued, "We want to have a reason to keep watching Evron. We don't want him completely free while we are waiting for her case to come to trial."

"Well, I guess we have to let you do your job." Mom looked at me. "Dani?"

I nodded and took a deep breath and retold the story. Mom held my hand while I relived the worst moment of my life. Mills wrote down notes. When I was done, the room was quiet. Benny was sleeping, and I was thankful to have Mom baby me.

After a few minutes, Mills stopped reading his notes. He looked up and frowned, "Are you sure there is nothing else?"

I shook my head. Then suddenly an image appeared to me. I was upset by the memory. Mom put her arm around my shoulder. "What is it, baby?"

"Stupid really." I shifted and tried to shake off the memory.

"Dani, please let me decide if it's important or not." Mills didn't push me. He waited.

I finally spoke. "The car smelled like perfume. Strong perfume. Also, the back of my head hit a pile of small boxes." I looked at my hands. "They were boxes of new condoms." I took a deep breath. "I know it's weird, but he never used a condom with me when we … you know … before that night. Why would he have so many?"

I looked up just in time to see the look on Mills's face. It was small, but it was there. A tiny smile crossed Mill's lips. "Thank you, Dani." He got up to leave. He shook both our hands. "Thank you, Jasmeet." He looked back at me. "I know it's hard to believe, but we are trying to do our best to help you. Trust me, Dani."

"I'm trying," I whispered.

CHAPTER 31

April

There was one tree that stood in front of our building. It was alone. I never really noticed it before. I had Benny in my arms, and we were on our way to meet Mrs. Elpidia. Benny yelled, "Ellow." His fingers were pointing at the tree.

I stopped and smiled. "Yes, Benny. It is yellow." The buds were small, but the yellow was still there. A warm feeling spread across my body. I kissed my brother. He made me see things I no longer saw.

I turned toward the bus stop when I was stopped by a tall figure. "I like that tree too." Keon smiled.

I was surprised to see him. "What are you doing home?"

"Good to see you too," he teased.

I felt myself blush. "I'm sorry. I'm not used to seeing you except at night." Then I looked away. "That didn't sound right." I just stood there looking down.

Keon laughed. He tried to touch my arm, but I pulled away. I always pulled away. He stopped laughing. "Why do you keep doing that?"

I looked up at him. I felt the lump in my throat begin to grow, but I didn't give in to it. "I don't know." I was telling the truth.

We stood there in silence while Benny kept saying, "Ellow, ellow."

Finally Keon whispered in my ear, "I am not Evron."

I looked into his eyes and saw something. He was sad and calm at the same time. Almost like he felt pity for me. He looked down and started to walk away.

"Keon," I said, waiting for him to turn around. When he looked at me I was finally able to say, "I know. I know you are not Evron. But knowing isn't the same as feeling."

He nodded and came up and kissed Benny. His lips had never been that close to me. "Let me know, Dani, when you can feel the difference."

CHAPTER 32

The Promise

I started to listen to Mrs. Elpidia. I knew she understood me more than anyone else. That really helped. Sometimes we just talked about movies or music. Sometimes we talked about Dad leaving or Mom's fling with Ted. Sometimes she taught me how to play chess. A lot of the time she just let me cry.

"What if I never get better?" I asked her as I moved a pawn in a game of chess. "What if I always think of Evron when Keon … or anyone touches me?"

Mrs. Elpidia lifted up her bishop and knocked over my queen. She smiled.

"Dani, whatever happens, life will go on." She paused, taking my queen off the board. She looked at me and said, "And you can handle it. I promise."

The way she said it made me believe her.

CHAPTER 33

Moving Out

Keon sent me a text when I got home. "I was home today because I'm moving out. Will let you know where. Will still ride bus with you. Let me know nights you don't go to school," he wrote.

I read the text at least ten times before I put it down. How could he move? If he wasn't with Ruth and Evron, then who would keep them from coming after me?

I could still hear Mrs. Elpidia's words. "Life will go on," she said. But I wasn't sure if I could handle it.

I quickly texted back. "You can't! I need you!"

It only took a minute before Keon responded. "Good to know ☺"

His response made me smile. Maybe I did feel the difference between the two brothers. Maybe Keon had to move. He wanted to make sure that I could not only know and feel the difference, but also see it.

CHAPTER 34

Behind

It didn't seem to matter if I was getting missed assignments and notes from Eva or not. My grades were slipping.

"Miss Garcia, may I speak with you please." My teacher pulled me aside as Eva and I were heading out the door. I told Eva I'd be right there.

I walked up to the man who was my last chance at finishing high school. "Sir?"

"Miss Garcia, you have missed too many hours. You must miss no more hours or you will be unable to earn the credits." He spoke to me like I was an adult. He thought I was an adult. He thought I had a choice. He was wrong.

"Sir, I am getting the work from Eva. I am doing the best I can. Please. Please, help me." I looked at Eva who was pointing at the bus stop. I had to go or I would miss my bus. "Sir, I have to watch my baby brother while my mother works." I looked at him one last time.

"I have heard everything before." He was not mean. He was stating facts. "I have to stick to the rules. I cannot bend. Otherwise I would be graduating a lot of empty desks." He turned and left.

"Dani!" I heard Eva yell. "Hurry up!"

I ran to get on the bus as Eva held the door open. The bus driver cursed once and then closed the door. I sat by a window and waved to Eva. She couldn't hear me, but I still said, "Thank you."

I tried to push the sinking feeling away again as I looked out the bus window. The night lights made the streets look like

Christmas all year long. I used to smile at the lights when I was younger. I felt like I lived in a special place. At night the filth of the streets disappeared. At night the lights promised magic. At night I would feel the city's energy. But I had lost that feeling. I longed to be that young girl again.

The lights became a blur. I couldn't believe I was stuck again. I wiped my face before we hit the Market Place. I didn't want to cry anymore. I wanted to be in control.

Keon sat next to me as always. This time he let his leg slowly lean against mine. It took me a few minutes to even notice. He was touching me, but it was as normal as Benny sitting on my lap, or Mom kissing the top of my head. I didn't pull away.

"I think I'm done with school. So you won't need to take me home anymore." My voice sounded like a little girl. "You can go straight to your new place now."

Keon turned his head. "What are you talking about? You're so close to graduating."

I told him about what the teacher said. I turned my head away so he wouldn't see my tears. Life will go on. I tried to repeat the words in my head. Life will go on. But I didn't believe it.

"I moved to the apartments next to the Market Place," said Keon. "I'm in 304. You can visit when you want."

"Thanks." I wiped my face with my sleeve.

We didn't say much else. But the warmth from his leg gave me strength. I didn't want the bus ride to end.

As Keon walked me to my door, he smiled. "Look Dani, you are strong. Don't give up on school. Think! Think hard about what you can do to make it happen. There has got to be something you haven't thought about."

CHAPTER 35

Crossing Paths

Two months. That's how long it was before I saw Evron again. Two months! I had managed to turn him into a monster. He was eight feet tall, hairy with fangs. At least that was how I felt about him. My feelings had created a monster. I was sure he would eat me alive.

But when I saw Evron, I almost missed the chance meeting. I was on the bus on my way to Mrs. Elpidia's. The bus stopped at the same building where Ruth got out a few weeks before. I let my head turn because I saw someone I knew. I almost didn't recognize Evron. His hair was cut short, and he had his arm wrapped around a girl. I should say a woman. I couldn't really tell. She was dressed like Ruth had been. She was ready to party.

For one moment Evron's head turned, and he saw me. His arm dropped, and he turned his whole body toward the bus. I turned away. I didn't want to look long enough to let his eyes cut into me.

As the bus started to turn the corner, I dared to look outside again. This time I saw a cop car. I didn't think anything at first. We always had cops moving around the blocks. But then I quickly looked again. It was Officer James. I hadn't seen him since he was in my hospital room with the detective. He was just sitting in the car. He looked in Evron's direction. Then he picked up his two-way radio and spoke into it.

I didn't see anything else. The bus had moved on. A smile grew from somewhere deep inside of me. Maybe the police had not forgotten about Evron. Maybe Detective Mills was telling me the truth. Maybe they were watching Evron. Maybe he couldn't hurt me again even if he wanted to. I took a deep breath and looked forward to seeing Mrs. Elpidia.

CHAPTER 36
New Plan

Mrs. Grady?" I whispered as I stood in the doorway to Mrs. Grady's classroom. I had slipped into my old school hoping to see my old teacher. It was lunchtime and she was sitting at her desk.

She smiled and put down a sandwich. She walked over to me with her arms wide open. She hugged me and kissed Benny. "My dear Dani. Sweet Benny. How are you doing?"

I told her how Mom was working longer hours for Ted. I told her I had to stop my night classes. I told her I was not going to graduate.

Mrs. Grady's little lips got tight. She shut her eyes a little, like she was looking really hard. "I don't think so, young lady!" She was almost angry.

"Please don't be angry with me!" I stood back. I didn't understand her crazy reaction. I didn't have a choice. "I came here because I have run out of options."

She walked back over to her desk. She sat down on the edge like she was holding herself up. "You came to the right place." Mrs. Grady's voice had softened. "I am not angry with you." She shook her head. "It's Ted!"

"Ted?" I was confused.

Mrs. Grady walked back over to me and pulled me away from the door and shut it behind me. She sat down on the edge of a desk again. I let Benny get down and scoot around. "I need to ask you something." She looked really serious. "I think I know the answer, but I have to be sure."

I looked at her for a long minute before I said, "Sure. What is it?"

I could see a look that wasn't questioning, but almost hoping, "Is Benny Ted's son?"

I thought the question was too personal. But Mrs. Grady had helped me. I trusted her. "Yes, he is. But Ted doesn't want to admit it."

A smile grew. Tears flowed. With her hand on her chest she moved over to pick up Benny. He giggled. She kissed him. I stared. "I knew it! I knew it!" Mrs. Grady repeated.

"Then let me know it!" I finally said. I had both hands on my hips.

The overjoyed woman looked at me. "That good-for-nothing Ted is my son. This means …"

"Benny is your grandson," I finished. I couldn't explain how I felt. The whole thing was too strange. It took a few minutes before I felt anything. It was like my brain had to make connections. Ted … Mom … Benny ... teacher … not teacher ... grandmother. Finally, I felt a smile cross my face. "That means you're my grandmother in a mixed-up sort of way?"

Mrs. Grady took my hand. "I can be." She kissed Benny again. "With your mother's permission, I'd like to start seeing my grandson."

I fumbled around to find my phone and gave Mrs. Grady Mom's number. "I'm sure Mom will freak out at first. But she'll get over it. I'll remind her about what a great teacher you've been."

Mrs. Grady laughed at my awkward self. "Thanks, Dani. But here's the thing." Her face got serious again. "I want to see him tonight and each night you have school while your mom works."

Suddenly the final connection was made. She would make graduating happen. She was my new plan.

CHAPTER 37

May

It didn't take Mom long to fall in love with Mrs. Grady. Benny fell in love with his grandma too. Sometimes he cried when she left.

I was back at school. Mrs. Grady would often come early enough for me to head to school early. This way I could meet up and visit with Eva. Eva made me laugh about stupid things. She didn't talk about sex like it was candy to be handed out freely. She spoke of her crush on the hot guy in the front row. If he looked at her, she'd melt.

I loved being around Eva. She made plans. She made plans for when she graduated. She got a job smack in the middle of downtown, where the big businesses looked down over the rest of the world. She said it was only a mailroom job, but it would help pay for college if she took one class at a time.

Eva made me think. She made me think about my future. Somehow I only pictured myself raising Benny. But I didn't have to keep thinking that anymore. Not since Grandma Grady took over.

I knew I would not get the college scholarship. I had missed too many days to pull up my grades. But maybe I could take a class at a time like Eva. I would just need to find a job first.

CHAPTER 38

High

I was on high. Hope flooded my body. As long as I didn't think about Evron, I could feel my fear slip away. My life was moving on, a little at a time. Mrs. Elpidia was right.

The ride home on the bus was relaxed. Keon told me about his new place and how it was good to be out of the family apartment.

"Do you miss Ruth and your mom?" I didn't even want to say Evron's name.

Keon looked out the window. "I miss the family I used to have." I didn't say anything. I just let him talk when he was ready. "Mom is working hard, but she's gone all the time. I think she takes on more hours, so she doesn't have to be at home. She only sleeps and eats there. Sometimes not even that. Some weeks she's gone for days." He looked at me and sighed. "I don't recognize Evron and Ruth anymore. We used to laugh all the time. Now … well, I can only imagine what they are up to." He gave me a half smile. "They are old enough now that they don't need me. They won't listen to me anyway."

"What about money?" I asked. I was not sure if that was too personal.

Keon didn't seem to mind. He laughed a little. "I told Evron that if he had enough money to spend on his clothes and phones, then he could start paying the rent." I didn't say anything. Keon sighed. "I'm happy to go home now and not have to block out Ruth and Evron yelling at each other. It's only getting worse." He leaned his head against the window. "Yeah, I miss my old family."

I slowly reached out and touched Keon's fingers. I slid my fingers between his and drank up his warmth. His hand eagerly wrapped around mine. He lifted his head and looked at me. His eyes asked a ton of questions, but he said nothing.

I smiled and whispered, "I know *and feel* you are not Evron."

CHAPTER 39

Old Friend

The stairwell was empty as always. I told Keon I could walk to the door on my own. He didn't kiss me, but I could tell he wanted to. I smiled as I watched him walk away. I almost skipped to my front door.

Just as I felt the cold knob in my hand, I heard a whimper. I looked up the stairs and could make out some feet. Someone was sitting on the stairs just out of sight.

"Hello?" I called out. My heart was pounding as memories came flooding back.

"Dani?" Ruth's voice cried. She sounded like she was ten. She sounded like she did when we were friends. She sounded afraid.

I slowly let go of the door knob and started up the stairs. I told myself I was stupid. I should run into the apartment. But I couldn't. I was pulled to the voice. I was pulled by the sound of a friend who used to care. "Ruth?" I called out. "Are you okay?"

I turned the corner and saw my old friend. She was dressed in high heels and a miniskirt. From the angle she was sitting, I could see she wasn't wearing underwear. Her make-up was all smeared. Tears flowed down her face. She reached for me. I didn't come close at first. But a deep cry coming from her pulled me in to catch her arms. She cried and then turned her head to puke. She wiped her mouth and tried to breathe.

"What happened?" I asked. I took her small jacket and wiped her mouth.

She just looked at me. Her eyes looked so empty. She slowly reached up to mock pinch my cheek. She whispered, "I didn't say no." A sick laugh gushed from deep inside her.

"What are you talking about?" I sat down next to her, careful to avoid the puke.

She stopped laughing and rested her head on my shoulder. "Dani, I'm so tired." I didn't know what to say, so I just sat there. She spoke to me like we had never stopped being friends. "It's Evron."

Horror struck through me. "He didn't …"

"Oh, no!" She stopped me. "He didn't rape me. Not like he raped you." It was the first time I heard her take the blame away from me. It was the first time she accused her brother. "But he might as well have."

"What do you mean?" She didn't move her head. It was like a weight too heavy to bear anymore.

"He pimped me out." She said it like a cuss word that she'd been holding back a long time. "He has been for a long time.

First it was his friends, and then kids at school." She paused. "Then when you were not around anymore, he took me uptown."

"That building?" I asked. Suddenly her dress and make-up all made sense. I felt stupid for not having seen it before. A prostitution ring? Is that what Detective Mills was talking about? I asked Ruth, "He pimps out others too, doesn't he?"

"Yeah." She was falling asleep. I gently put down her head and ran to my apartment. I caught Grandma Grady checking on Benny. She told me to be quiet but quickly saw I needed her. She followed me out the door and up the stairs. She tried to keep a cry from escaping her lips. But the sound filled the stairwell.

We carefully lifted Ruth. Grandma Grady helped me get her into my room. We undressed Ruth and cleaned her up.

The smell of alcohol and perfume was hard to get rid of, but we tried.

It wasn't long before we had Ruth settled. Grandma Grady looked at me and didn't have to say a thing. I reached for Detective Mills's number and made a call.

CHAPTER 40

Midnight

Detective Mills and Officer Jones showed up within the hour. We managed to wake up Ruth enough to make a statement. I wasn't sure how she would react when she saw the police, but I didn't care. It felt good not to worry about what she thought. I was taking charge.

She looked confused at first, but then she breathed a sigh of relief. It was like she was able to let go of an awful secret. They finally told me to bring her down to the station in the morning. She fell asleep quickly after they left.

When Mom came home, she freaked out. She paced around as we told her the story. She settled some when we told her the police had come by.

"Will you please stay?" Mom asked Grandma Grady as the little lady was gathering her items.

Grandma Grady's face lit up. She came over to Mom and took her into her thin little arms. Mom let her. "Of course, my dear Jasmeet. That's what grandmas are for."

"Thanks," Mom whispered. "You and Benny take my room."

Grandma Grady started to object, but Mom wouldn't listen to her.

Soon Mom was lying on the couch while I was stretched out on the floor. Grandma Grady was asleep in Mom's bed with Benny snuggled in her arms.

"Mom," I whispered.

"Yeah?" Her voice was tired. She was almost asleep.

"Do you think it's almost over?" I asked.

I could hear her shift her weight. "Yeah, baby. It's got to be."

"Good." I checked the clock on my phone. Midnight.

I could hear Mom begin to snore. I kept thinking about the evening and couldn't sleep. I was starting to put it all together. Now it made sense. Mills thought that the pile of condoms in the car was one more reason to believe he was giving them to his girls. To his hookers. To his sister. The thought of it all made my insides turn. I tried to think of other things. Like city lights. But the image of Ruth was hard to get out of my head.

Just as I began to doze off, I heard footsteps outside the door. Suddenly I heard banging. "Ruth! I know you're in there!" Evron's voice jerked me wide awake. Terror flooded my body once again.

Mom sat up and grabbed my arm. She whispered, "Don't move. If we don't answer, then he'll go away."

But the banging continued. This time you could feel him flinging his body against the door. He was trying to break it down.

Ruth and Grandma Grady came running into the room turning on the lights. Ruth cried, "Maybe I should go."

Grandma Grady touched Ruth's arm. "I don't think so, my dear." She winked and walked over to the door. She yelled as loud as she could. "Young man, I don't know who you think you are. But there is no Ruth here. I have just moved in and you must be very confused. If you keep banging, I will call the police. I have the phone in my hand right now." Her strange voice shut Evron up. He quickly ran up the stairs. Silence ruled once more.

CHAPTER 41

Not Over

I thought it was all over. With Ruth's statement I was sure the meeting at the police station would bring an end to Evron's crimes. Once again I was wrong.

I called Keon to meet us there. He looked awful. He hadn't shaved and his clothes were just thrown on. I'd never seen his clothes not match. He ran up to hug Ruth. She looked pretty good. My old friend was relaxed in my way too big blue jeans and sweatshirt. I could see she loved the warmth and safety of my clothes. I smiled at her.

Keon just held Ruth. They didn't say much. I guess they didn't know what to say.

Mom and Grandma Grady stood with us as we waited to see Detective Mills. The lady at the front desk finally told us to sit down. We walked over to the old plastic chairs. We were not alone. But it felt like we were.

It wasn't long before Detective Mills showed us into a room with a long table. It was big enough to fit all of us. Mills sat on the far end with a pile of papers in front of him. I sat between Mom and Ruth with Keon sitting on the other side of Ruth, holding her hand. Keon's jaw was set. He looked angry. Once in a while he'd wipe away a tear.

Mom couldn't stand the silence. "Well, have you grabbed the boy yet? How much more pain is Evron going to dish out and get away with?" That was not the best way to start the meeting, but I didn't blame her. We were all thinking it.

Detective Mills didn't seem upset by Mom's comment. "Mrs. Garcia, I mean Jasmeet, you are right. It is time to bring Evron in again." Mom leaned back in her chair nodding. Mills continued, "He already has a rape charge against him. As you know, we are waiting for that to come to trial." There were a few choice curse words dropped. For a moment I thought they might have come from Grandma Grady. But it was not a time for me to be shocked.

"Well?" Keon said.

Mills quickly focused again, "But now we may add a charge of running a prostitution ring."

"But aren't the rape charges more serious?" Keon was leaning forward in his chair.

"Yes, but ..." Mills looked at Ruth for

a moment. "With Ruth testifying about the young age at which he started pimping her out …" Ruth dropped her head into her hands. Mills continued, "We could charge him with sex crimes against children. With all of the charges, Evron could face many years in prison."

"Then arrest him!" Mom said, but it almost sounded like a question.

Detective Mills paused for a moment. "A wire tap could be the final hard evidence."

"What?" Mom was standing. She walked up behind Ruth. "We will not have Ruth face her brother again." She gently touched Ruth's shoulders.

Mills took a sip of coffee. "We have enough evidence to get a court order for wiring a conversation."

"Between who?" Keon asked.

Ruth started to cry. Grandma Grady walked her out of the room. She fired a few more choice words. She was on fire.

Mills watched them leave and then looked at me. "Would you be willing, Dani?" My heart about jumped out of my skin.

"No way!" Mom was still standing. She came up behind me. "My baby will not face that man again."

Mills started moving around the papers on the table, "I was hoping Ruth or Dani would confront him. But I guess we'll have to use the evidence we have."

"I'll do it." Keon's voice was like ice.

Mills looked at him and frowned. "I'm not sure how that would help. You have not been part of this …"

"Exactly!" Keon's jaw was still tight. "It's time I'm part of this. I'll do what I need to do to stop Evron." Keon paused. "Even if he is my brother."

CHAPTER 42
Waiting

I thought time couldn't go any slower. Keon and the police had to wait for the perfect moment. It never seemed to come. Keon had to find a logical reason to meet with Evron. But he had made it clear when he moved out that he wasn't coming back. He had to find a way to make it happen.

Ruth took off to live with Grandma Grady on the other side of town. She was safe there, for now. She'd call me and tell me how she couldn't quite get over all the stares she got. A young black girl moving into an all-white neighborhood made some cars slow down. Grandma

Grady just laughed it off as good for the neighborhood.

"I miss home," Ruth said on the phone one afternoon. Grandma Grady was at school, and I was watching Benny.

"It's just for a few weeks," I said, not really getting her. "How can you want to come home with Evron still on the streets?"

There was a long pause. Finally she said, "I miss what I know." She took a bite of something crunchy before she explained herself. "I mean, I miss my room and my streets and my friends." She laughed a little. "But I don't miss that awful stink from the garbage that piles up behind the playground."

We laughed and it felt good.

CHAPTER 43
Ready

think I'm ready." I sat across from Mrs. Elpidia. She was looking down at the chess board.

She didn't look up. "For what?"

"To move on." I said like it was nothing. "I think I am over the attack."

Mrs. Elpidia looked at me. I thought she would smile, but she didn't. She just looked. "Really?" She glanced at the chess board again. She made a move and looked at me. "So tell me about why you feel that way."

It had been over a month since she sounded like a counselor. Suddenly she did again. I tried not to show that I was bothered by her tone. I looked down at the board and took her bishop with my queen. I looked up and said, "Look, Mrs. Elpidia. I am thankful for all you've done. But I think I'm okay now. The police are getting ready to arrest Evron. Then I'll be good."

She held my stare. "So let me get this straight. You are okay about your rape because the police are about to pick up Evron?"

I frowned. "When you say it that way, it sounds lame." I was not sure why I was getting mad. But I was. "Don't you want me to get better?" I was a little louder than I should have been.

Mrs. Elpidia almost whispered. "What does *better* mean?" Her counseling voice was setting me off. Way off!

"That's a stupid question!" I yelled.

"*Then answer it*!" Her voice was loud and firm.

I stood up, bumping the board. The chess pieces moved out of position. Our game was over. I didn't care. I looked at her with tears in my eyes. "I guess it means that I don't think of the rape every day and night. I guess it means I can walk down the street without fear creeping up behind me when there is nothing there. I guess it means that I can take control of my life."

There was a moment of silence before she asked, "Do you do all those things?"

Tears fell freely. "No." It was the hardest word I have ever had to say. I added, "But I'm trying. It's not as bad as it was."

"Good!" Mrs. Elpidia started setting up the board again. "Then you are getting better." She smiled at me. "My dear, you have always been on the edge of ready. You are simply practicing it every day until one day it becomes a part of who you are. But that day will be a long time from now. It's not something that is gone just because someone is locked up."

I sat down and helped set up the chess pieces. I looked at this beautiful woman in front of me. "But you got over it." I wanted to be her.

"Did I?" She looked at me. Something lifted inside of me. It was like a lightness that I had not ever felt. I finally got what Mrs. Elpidia was saying. I would never forget the rape. But, like her, I could and would become whole again.

CHAPTER 44

Graduation

My perfect day. I was waiting for this day since I started school. Mom had promised me this day would happen. It had finally arrived.

It was a small graduation. We held it outside the building where we attended our night classes. Eva and I looked like twins in our black robes and square hats. Grandma Grady was able to stand with our teacher and help hand out diplomas. She reached out and hugged me as I came through the line. She whispered, "I knew you could do it."

I whispered back, "Because of you." I could see tears well up in my old teacher's eyes.

Our teeth couldn't have been bigger or whiter as we smiled while Mom took hundreds of pictures. Keon and Ruth were dressed up and handing out hugs like free popcorn. Eva enjoyed meeting Keon and Ruth. I was so happy.

As we rode the bus home from graduation, Keon sat next to me. I had taken off my black robe to show off my new red dress. The only dress I had. My hair still looked good. Mom had done her best to form perfect curls flowing in every direction. They were held in place with enough gel that I wondered if they'd ever come out. I didn't feel fat or ugly. I felt beautiful.

I wanted Keon to come to the apartment with us and eat food Grandma Grady had ordered from the Market Place. I'd never seen that much food before.

Right before his stop Keon looked at me. He touched my hand and kissed the top of my head. "I am so proud of you. But I got to go. Got something I got to do."

He got off the bus, and I watched him head off toward his apartment. I hadn't been there yet. I wanted to. I smiled at the thought and looked at Mom. She was watching me and smiled back.

I moved over to her seat and whispered, "Mom, I know you have all that food. But maybe I can get out at the next stop and walk back to get Keon to join us."

Mom patted my leg. "Sure, baby, it's your graduation. If you want Keon there, you should go get him."

The bus let me out two blocks down. I smiled as the bus took off. I could hear Ruth and Mom whistling at me out the window.

I turned to walk the few blocks, for the

first time thinking of nothing else but that perfect day.

I turned to head into Keon's building. I opened the door to go up the stairs. My heart stopped. I was staring into Evron's eyes.

CHAPTER 45
Timing

Hey, baby." Evron's voice was clear and in control. I stood still, unable to move. He moved in close and touched my hair. He traced a curl as far down as it would go. "You look good. Who you dressed up for?"

"Nobody," I barely whispered. "I graduated today."

I could feel his breath on my mouth. "Oh, you smell good. Graduated. That means you're a big girl. I miss you, baby." He kissed my ear. I felt myself wanting to puke.

Somewhere deep down I felt Mrs. Elpidia's voice. Move on. I wanted to scream at her—how could I move on if he was in my face? I took a deep breath and felt my arm come up. I felt myself touch his face and push him away. "*Stop it!*" I yelled and looked right into his eyes. I know he saw my fear. But he also saw something else.

He pushed my hand down and started for me again. I backed up enough to put a distance between us. "Come on, baby." He grabbed my arm and pulled me toward the back of the stairwell. I was hoping someone would show up.

"Let go of me now!" I said and kicked him in between the legs as hard as I could.

He let go of me, and I ran for the door. Just as I pushed it open, I heard footsteps.

"Dani?" Keon's voice made me stop. "What are you doing here?"

I turned to face him. "I was coming to get you, but then …" I looked in Evron's direction. He was still holding his groin.

Keon's eyes changed. I could see anger

rise, and he started to head for his brother. He suddenly stopped and looked at me. "What happened?"

I thought it was a weird question. I was ticked now. "What does it look like? Evron tried to attack me again. He started to pull me behind the stairs, but I kicked him. I kicked him good."

Stumbling around a little, Evron tried to walk. He looked at Keon with a fake smile. "She sure did!" Evron tried to laugh. "Hey, brother. I thought I was coming up to your place?" He tried to touch his brother's shoulder.

Keon pushed Evron's arm away. "I thought so too, but it looks like you had to get you some before you came up." Keon's voice was like ice.

Evron stood up taller now. The laughter was gone. He met Keon's stare. "She ain't nothin', Keon. You know family is everything."

"Is that what you told Ruth?" Keon asked. His eyes never left Evron's.

"She knew what she was doing," Evron said as if it were a fact. "She never said she didn't want all those men."

Keon's jaw was flexing. "Is that right? Even when she was fourteen, you hooked her up. Didn't you? You think she could tell you no? She loved you. She trusted you. And you used her."

I could tell he wanted to punch Evron. I wanted him to punch Evron. I didn't get why he didn't.

"Sure I did. It was easy." Evron walked in closer, realizing his brother wasn't going to hit him. "Once I realized I could get money for Ruth, I realized I didn't have to work like a dog. Like you." He almost spat in Keon's face. "I saw how hard you worked. For what?" He walked around Keon and looked at me. Then he said, "All for what? So you can have my leftovers?"

Tears began to flood my eyes. Why didn't Keon punch him? I was just about to kick him when I saw Keon look at me. He looked beyond Evron's words. He looked beyond my hurt. He looked into me. His eyes said trust me.

"So you rape Dani, and then you start pimping out other girls along with your sister?" Keon's words made it all too clear to me what was happening. He was wired. This was it. This was the moment I had been waiting for. I just didn't think I would be part of it. I was never supposed to be a part of it. Keon didn't tell me. He didn't want to ruin my graduation. He didn't want to ruin my day.

I tried not to show my sudden change. I turned my head because I knew I couldn't act like Keon could. Evron walked over and grabbed my face. I closed my eyes. I didn't want to betray the moment. I was still shaking, which I thought was good.

Evron finally answered, "Raping Dani was not worth it." And he flung my face away. He walked back over to his brother who was still controlling his anger. He pulled out the biggest wad of money I had ever seen. He waved it in front of his brother's face. "Pimping out girls and Ruth … worth it."

At that moment Keon stood up. He walked over to me and put his arms around me. "Let's go to your graduation party, Dani." We walked out the door.

Evron came running out. "What? You can't just walk away from me like that!"

Keon stopped and looked back one last time. "Oh, yes I can." We both turned and headed to the bus stop. Detective Mills and Officer Jones came out of a nearby van. They had two other officers with them. As soon as Evron saw them he cursed and started running. The two other officers took only moments to catch up with him.

As Keon and I sat down at the bus stop, he reached over to grab my hand. "I know this was hard for you. But the timing was perfect. I was going to do it on my own, but you showing up made it work. Made it real."

"It was real to me." I looked at him. "I'm lucky you came down."

"Not luck." Keon smiled. He pointed at the van. "Mills saw you come in and warned me."

CHAPTER 46

June

Evron wasn't able to get out on bond. He had been arrested for a second crime while out on bail for the first crime. The court set the bail at ten grand. Even Evron's small prostitution ring couldn't pay for it. Since it was so much and it was secured, he didn't have any friends or family willing to put up the cash. I didn't feel sorry for him.

I knew Evron's arrest was not the end. I knew it was the beginning of a long trial. I knew I would still have to face him. But I also knew that I could do it.

While the waiting game began again, I started to look for a job.

"Why don't you work at the Market Place," Keon asked me one day as we took Benny to play on the small playground next to our building. One swing was still good and the slide was still standing. Keon kept putting Benny at the top of the slide while I caught him at the bottom.

"I don't know if I can." I wasn't so sure they would even talk to me. "I haven't worked a job since Benny was born. Before that I did odd jobs that I could pick up and drop as I needed to. That's not too good of a record."

Keon laughed. "I think finishing school is a pretty good record." He put Benny at the top of the slide again. "Besides, I'll put a good word in for you. I've got connections." He raised his eyebrows like he was important. I laughed and caught the giggling Benny at the bottom of the slide.

"Okay." I smiled. "I'll see if they will talk to me. It would be great to get a steady job. Maybe I could start a college class at the community college in the fall."

"I have an idea." Keon's face was a little more serious than I liked. "You could save on bus fare and move in with me. I'm closer to the college and work."

I stopped moving and almost missed catching Benny. A part of me was trying to figure out what Keon just said. But I waited too long to respond. He quickly added, "Or maybe not." He started to move toward the one bench near the slide.

"Wait," I said. I grabbed Benny up in my arms. He didn't like it much.

Benny yelled, "Side, side!" My little brother was getting stronger. He kept pulling his body in the direction of the slide. My arms began to hurt.

I walked over to Keon. "It's just I don't know what that means!" I felt stupid. But that was the best way to explain it. We weren't in a relationship. He had never kissed me. Now suddenly I would be living with him? What about Benny? What about Mom? I didn't know how to explain all these feelings to him.

He just looked at me and smiled softly. "It means I want to give you a chance to get out. To break away from falling back into your old habits." He lifted his hands. "I promise, no strings attached."

I tried to get Benny to stop yelling but I couldn't. I started throwing him in the air. He finally started giggling. I sat down next to Keon. I wasn't sure what he meant by habits. I thought I was doing my best. He made it sound bad. I knew he wanted to keep helping me, but I wasn't ready for a move. "You have done so much for me. I just need to start feeling like I can do life again on my own. Besides, Mom still needs me."

"Does she?" Keon's voice was serious. "Or do you just want to stay at home?"

"What's that supposed to mean?" I could feel myself begin to get angry. Benny tried pulling me off the bench toward the slide again.

Keon reached for Benny, but I turned him away. Keon frowned and said, "It means you say you want to control your life and move on, but you really can't! You have to stick to what you know. You're afraid of what else might be out there for you." Keon stood up and walked away. I stood up too and held Benny as he screamed.

Anger burst from my lips like fire. I turned and yelled, *"What do you know?"* After I said it I felt stupid. I walked toward the slide again. Benny stopped screaming. I kept turning my head to look at Keon. I was hoping he would come back. I was hoping he'd play with Benny again. But he didn't.

Before he reached the bus stop he looked back once. He had a sad look on his face, and then just shook his head. I felt like a child. I felt like I was missing something. I just didn't know what.

CHAPTER 47

Habits

Habits. What did he mean by that? I had to help Mom. I had to make sure Benny would be okay. I had to. I knew that I could help Mom. I also knew I could get a job and start classes. I was going to show Keon I could control my life. This meant I would still be able to help Mom. I thought helping family and helping yourself were good habits. What did Keon know?

The summer heat didn't help with job hunting. I spent my days walking into shops all sweaty and gross. By the time I was interviewed, I was wiping my face on my sleeve. I didn't go to the Market Place.

I wanted to do this without Keon. I would show him.

I finally got a job as a cashier at the Super Store about thirty minutes away. I was able to get the evening shift, so I could watch Benny during the day while Mom worked. It was working out. Grandma Grady would watch Benny at least once a week. She loved it.

It was working out. At least it did for two weeks.

"Dani," Mom said. She came into my room and woke me up before she headed for work. "I need you to watch Benny to-night." She turned and headed out my door.

I sat up straight in bed. I was suddenly wide awake. "What?" I followed her out into the living room. "I can't. I'm working. I can't start missing work. They'll fire me."

Mom walked up to me and flattened down my messed up hair. "Baby, I'm sure you can miss one time."

"Why?" I was feeling anger rise. I was feeling an old life creep back up on me. One that I thought was over. "Why do you need me to miss work?"

"I have a date." Her eyes danced.

"What?" I was shocked. "With who?"

"Ted," she giggled. "He said he was listening to his mom and wants to get to know Benny. He thought maybe we could talk about it over dinner."

"Then take Benny!" I was *not* happy.

Mom looked at me almost like she was getting upset. "What? You don't want me to work things out with Benny's father?"

I lifted my arms. "Oh, no. Don't you make this something I have to fix." Suddenly I got it. This was what Keon was talking about. I was always fixing Mom's problems. I was bending and almost breaking to make life work for her. I started laughing.

"What's so funny?" Mom was confused.

I took a breath and looked at her. For the first time in my life I felt sorry for Mom. "Look, Mom. You figure this one out. I'm going to work tonight."

"But ..." I heard Mom's voice trail off as I closed my door.

CHAPTER 48

Next

I found out later Mom did take Benny. It was a good thing. Mom could tell it would be a long time before Ted would be comfortable with Benny. She came home less excited. Reality hit her. He was never going to be her prince. But maybe he could be Benny's father. Time would tell.

I, on the other hand, decided to move out. Mom wasn't happy, but I was ready for the change. I told her I would help with Benny some, but she'd have to figure out the days I couldn't. I wasn't going to leave her totally hanging. But I also knew Grandma Grady would help out as much as she could.

I thought it would be easy to find a place to live. Wrong again. I soon found out I couldn't afford to live on my own. Ruth was back at her place with her mother, who suddenly found more time to be home. There was no way I wanted to move in with them. Grandma Grady offered to give me a room. But I wasn't ready for an all-white neighborhood. Then there was Eva. She had found a place on the other side of town with relatives. It would be faster for her to get downtown to her new job. I would miss her, but she said she'd keep in touch. I didn't have any other friends I could move in with except Keon.

Something stirred inside of me. I missed him. I told myself that I didn't want to move in with him. I told myself that I could live without him. I told myself that he was just a friend. But then I stopped. I smiled. I knew better.

CHAPTER 49

First Kiss

I stood in front of the meat section at the Market Place. "Hi."

Keon looked up from putting turkey into the display case. He looked surprised. But in a good way. "Hi, Dani. What's up?"

I looked around like I was looking for some meat. I was really looking for what to say next. "Not much," I lied. I was bursting to tell him how right he was, but I was standing in front of other customers wanting their ham.

"So, you need some meat?" Keon asked, not knowing what to say.

I looked at him and smiled, "Do you

have a special on, Keon?" I felt stupid after I said it, but it made him laugh.

He looked at the clock and said, "If you wait fifteen minutes, I'll be out for my lunch."

I nodded and headed to the benches at the front of the store. I sat next to a little old man waiting for his wife to finish shopping. He held a single rose in his hand. He'd spent the extra money in the flower section. Soon a little old lady with a freshly stacked beehive hairdo came up. The man smiled at her as he handed her the rose and took the groceries out of her hands. She smiled at him and kissed him gently. I watched them leave and whispered, "How sweet."

"Sure is." Keon's voice surprised me. "Don't see love like that often."

We walked out the door and found a spot outside. The bench was nasty with gum stuck in the corners. But we sat anyways. It was hot, but I didn't blame Keon for wanting a few minutes outside. We watched the old couple slowly walk to their car. I smiled at him. "I got a job at the Super Store."

He gently shoved my arm. "That's great."

There was a long pause before I finally said it. "You were right."

Keon played dumb. "About what?"

I gave him a fake mean stare. "You're going to make me say it, aren't you?"

"Yep." He crossed his arms and stuck his nose in the air. He was going to rub it in.

"You were right about my life," I started. "I was stuck. I was living my mom's life and not mine." I looked at him and smiled. "So I'm ready to move. You still need a roommate?"

Keon's smug look changed. He was suddenly serious. "Are you sure?"

I shook my head and told the truth. "No," I said. "But I've got to start somewhere."

We sat in silence. Keon's shoulders dropped. I could tell Keon wanted to ask me the question that hung between us. He just couldn't find the words. Finally he said, "I'm just a start?"

I hadn't chosen my words well. Keon wasn't a start for me. I shook my head at the poor choice of words, "Oh no, Keon. I didn't mean that."

He stood up to stretch. I could see that he was trying to play it cool. I didn't want this to be a replay of last month. He looked at me and sighed, "Then what do you mean?"

I stood up in front of him. Something about him always made me feel safe. "You are not my start. I really would like you to be my end." I pointed to the old couple that was just now pulling out of the parking lot. "Like them."

His look changed. I wouldn't say love, because I always saw that. He had never hidden his feelings of love for me. This was one of hope. "Are you sure?"

I touched his face gently. "I am." A tear fell down my cheek. "I'm just afraid."

He wrapped his arms around me and pulled me close. "Don't be." He smiled. "We'll take our sweet time."

That's when it happened. I had my first kiss. That first real one. The one that counts. The one that makes you feel like you are the most beautiful woman in the world. The one you hope will never stop. The one that makes you thankful you were born. The one that makes you believe nothing else can ever go wrong.

I wanted that moment to go on forever. I didn't want to face the fears that were still ahead. But I felt different. I knew now that I was stronger. I knew now that if ... I knew now that *when* I had to face anything else ... I could.